CW00481610

Words for the Wise

T. S. Arthur

WORDS FOR THE WISE.

BY

T. S. ARTHUR.

1851.

PREFACE.

THE title of this book—"WORDS FOR THE WISE"—is too comprehensive to need explanation. May the lessons it teaches be "sufficient" as warnings, incentives and examples, to hundreds and thousands who read them.

CONTENTS.

THE POOR DEBTOR.

"THERE is one honest man in the world, I am happy to say," remarked a rich merchant, named Petron, to a friend who happened to call in upon him.

"Is there, indeed! I am glad to find you have made a discovery of the fact. Who is the individual entitled to the honourable distinction?"

"You know Moale, the tailor?"

"Yes. Poor fellow! he's been under the weather for a long time."

"I know. But he's an honest man for all that."

"I never doubted his being honest, Mr. Petron."

"I have reason to know that he is. But I once thought differently. When he was broken up in business some years ago, he owed me a little bill, which I tried to get out of him as hard as any one ever did try for his own. But I dunned and dunned him until weary, and then, giving him up as a bad case, passed the trifle that he owed me to account of profit and loss. He has crossed my path a few times since; but, as I didn't feel toward him as I could wish to feel toward all men, I treated him with marked coldness. I am sorry for having done so, for it now appears that I judged him too severely. This morning he called in of his own free will, and paid me down the old account. He didn't say any thing about interest, nor did I, though I am entitled to, and ought to have received it. But, as long as he came forward of his own accord and settled his bill, after I had given up all hope of ever receiving it, I thought I might afford to be a little generous and not say any thing about the interest; and so I gave him a receipt in full. Didn't I do right?"

"In what respect?" asked the friend.

"In forgiving him the interest, which I might have claimed as well as not, and which he would, no doubt, have paid down, or brought me at some future time."

"Oh, yes. You were right to forgive the interest," returned the friend, but in a tone and with a manner that struck the merchant as rather singular. "No man should ever take interest on money due from an unfortunate debtor."

"Indeed! Why not?" Mr. Petron looked surprised. "Is not money always worth its interest?"

"So it is said. But the poor debtor has no money upon which to make an interest. He begins the world again with nothing but his ability to work; and, if saddled with an old debt—principal and interest—his case is hopeless. Suppose he owes ten thousand dollars, and, after struggling hard for three or four years, gets into a position that will enable him to pay off a thousand dollars a year. There is some chance for him to get out of debt in ten years. But suppose interest has been accumulating at the rate of some six hundred dollars a year. His debt, instead of being ten thousand, will have increased to over twelve thousand dollars by the time he is in a condition to begin to pay off any thing; and then, instead of being able to reduce the amount a thousand dollars a year, he will have to let six hundred go for the annual interest on the original debt. Four years would have to elapse before, under this system, he would get his debt down to where it was when he was broken up in business. Thus, at the end of eight years' hard struggling, he would not, really, have advanced a step out of his difficulties. A debt of ten thousand dollars would still be hanging over him. And if, persevering to the end, he should go on paying the interest regularly and reducing the principal, some twenty-five years of his life would be spent in getting free from debt, when little over half that time would have been required, if his creditors had, acting from the commonest dictates of humanity, voluntarily released the interest."

"That is a new view of the case, I must confess—at least new to me," said Mr. Petron.

"It is the humane view of the case. But, looking to interest alone, it is the best view for every creditor to take. Many a man who, with a little effort, might have cancelled, in time, the principal of a debt unfortunately standing against him, becomes disheartened at seeing it daily growing larger through the accumulation of interest, and gives up in despair. The desire to be free from debt spurs many a man into effort. But make the difficulties in his way so large as to appear insurmountable, and he will fold his hands in helpless inactivity. Thousands of dollars are lost every year in consequence of creditors grasping after too much, and breaking down the hope and energy of the debtors."

"Perhaps you are right," said Mr. Petron;—"that view of the case never presented itself to my mind. I don't suppose, however, the interest on fifty dollars would have broken down Moale."

"There is no telling. It is the last pound, you know, that breaks the camel's back. Five years have passed since his day of misfortune. Fifteen dollars for interest are therefore due. I have my doubts if he could have paid you sixty-five dollars now. Indeed, I am sure he could not. And the thought of that as a new debt, for which he had received no benefit whatever, would, it is more than probable, have produced a discouraged state of mind, and made him resolve not to pay you any thing at all."

"But that wouldn't have been honest," said the merchant.

"Perhaps not, strictly speaking. To be dishonest is from a set purpose to defraud; to take from another what belongs to him; or to withhold from another, when ability exists to pay, what is justly his due. You would hardly have placed Moale in either of these positions, if, from the pressure of the circumstances surrounding him as a poor man and in debt, he had failed to be as active, industrious, and prudent as he would otherwise have been. We are all apt to require too much of the poor debtor, and to have too little sympathy with him. Let the hope of improving your own condition—which is the mainspring of all your business operations—be taken away, and instead, let there be only the desire to pay off old debts through great labour and self-denial, that must continue for years, and imagine how differently you would think and feel from what you do now. Nay, more; let the debt be owed to those who are worth their thousands and tens of a thousands, and who are in the enjoyment of every luxury and comfort they could desire, while you go on paying them what you owe, by over-exertion and the denial to yourself and family of all those little luxuries and recreations which both so much need, and then say how deeply dyed would be that dishonesty which would cause you, in a moment of darker and deeper discouragement than usual, to throw the crushing weight from your shoulders, and resolve to bear it no longer? You must leave a man some hope in life if you would keep him active and industrious in his sphere."

Mr. Petron said nothing in reply to this; but he looked sober. His friend soon after left.

The merchant, as the reader may infer from his own acknowledgment, was one of those men whose tendency to regard only their own interests has become so confirmed a habit, that they can see nothing beyond the narrow circle of self. Upon debtors he had never looked with a particle of sympathy; and had, in all cases, exacted his own as rigidly as if his debtor had not been a creature of human wants and feelings. What had just been said, however, awakened a new thought in his mind; and, as he reflected upon the subject, he saw that there was some reason in what had been said, and felt half ashamed of his allusion to the interest of the tailor's fifty-dollar debt.

Not long after, a person came into his store, and from some cause mentioned the name of Moale.

"He's an honest man—that I am ready to say of him," remarked Mr. Petron.

"Honest, but very poor," was replied.

"He's doing well now, I believe," said the merchant.

"He's managing to keep soul and body together, and hardly that."

"He's paying off his old debts."

"I know he is; but I blame him for injuring his health and wronging his family, in order to pay a few hundred dollars to men a thousand times better off in the world than he is. He brought me twenty dollars on an old debt yesterday, but I wouldn't touch it. His misfortunes had long ago cancelled the obligation in my eyes. God forbid! that with enough to spare, I should take the bread out of the mouths of a poor man's children."

"Is he so very poor?" asked Mr. Petron, surprised and rebuked at what he heard.

"He has a family of six children to feed, clothe, and educate; and he has it to do by his unassisted labour. Since he was broken up in business some years ago, he has had great difficulties to contend

4

with, and only by pinching himself and family, and depriving both of nearly every comfort, has he been able to reduce the old claims that have been standing against him. But he has shortened his own life ten years thereby, and has deprived his children of the benefits of education, except in an extremely limited degree—wrongs that are irreparable. I honour his stern integrity of character, but think that he has carried his ideas of honesty too far. God gave him these children, and they have claims upon him for earthly comforts and blessings to the extent of his ability to provide. His misfortunes he could not prevent, and they were sent as much for the chastisement of those who lost by him as they were for his own. If, subsequently, his greatest exertion was not sufficient to provide more than ordinary comforts for the family still dependent upon him, his first duty was to see that they did not want. If he could not pay his old debts without injury to his health or wrong to his family, he was under no obligation to pay them; for it is clear, that no claims upon us are so imperative as to require us to wrong others in order to satisfy them."

Here was another new doctrine for the ears of the merchant—doctrine strange, as well as new. He did not feel quite so comfortable as before about the recovered debt of fifty dollars. The money still lay upon his desk. He had not yet entered it upon his cash-book, and he felt now less inclined to do so than ever. The claims of humanity, in the abstract, pressed themselves upon him for consideration, and he saw that they were not to be lightly thrust aside.

In order to pay the fifty dollars, which had been long due to the merchant, Mr. Moale had, as alleged, denied himself and family at every point, and overworked himself to a degree seriously injurious to his health; but his heart felt lighter after the sense of obligation was removed.

There was little at home, however, to make him feel cheerful. His wife, not feeling able to hire a domestic, was worn down with the care and labour of her large family; the children were, as a necessary consequence, neglected both in minds and bodies. Alas! there was no sunshine in the poor man's dwelling.

"Well, Alice," said Mr. Moale, as his wife came and stood by the board upon which he sat at work, holding her babe in her arms, "I have paid off another debt, thank heaven?"

"Whose?"

"Petron's. He believed me a rogue and treated me as such. I hope he thinks differently now."

"I wish all men were as honest in their intentions as you are."

"So do I, Alice. The world would be a much better one than it is, I am thinking."

"And yet, William," said his wife, "I sometimes think we do wrong to sacrifice so much to get out of debt. Our children" —

"Alice," spoke up the tailor, quickly, "I would almost sell my body into slavery to get free from debt. When I think of what I still owe, I feel as if I would suffocate."

"I know how badly you feel about it, William; but your heart is honest, and should not that reflection bear you up?"

"What is an honest heart without an honest hand, Alice?" replied the tailor, bending still to his work.

"The honest heart is the main thing, William; God looks at that. Man judges only of the action, but God sees the heart and its purposes."

"But what is the purpose without the act?"

"It is all that is required, where no ability to act is given. William, God does not demand of any one impossibilities."

"Though man often does," said the tailor, bitterly.

There was a pause, broken, at length, by the wife, who said—"And have you really determined to put John and Henry out to trades? They are so young."

"I know they are, Alice; too young to leave home. But" —

The tailor's voice became unsteady; he broke off in the middle of the sentence.

"Necessity requires it to be done," he said, recovering himself; "and it is of no avail to give way to unmanly weakness. But for this old debt, we might have been comfortable enough, and able to keep our children around us until they were of a more fitting age to go from under their parents' roof. Oh, what a curse is debt!"

"There is more yet to pay?"

"Yes, several hundreds of dollars; but if I fail as I have for a year past, I will break down before I get through."

"Let us think of our family, William; they have the first claim upon us. Those to whom money is owed are better off than we are; they stand in no need of it."

"But is it not justly due, Alice?" inquired the tailor, in a rebuking voice.

"No more justly due than is food, and raiment, and a *home* to our children," replied the tailor's wife, with more than her usual decision of tone. "God has given us these children, and he will require an account of the souls committed to our charge. Is not a human soul of more importance than dollars? A few years, and it will be out of our power to do our children good; they will grow up, and bear for ever the marks of neglect and wrong."

"Alice! Alice! for heaven's sake, do not talk in this way!" exclaimed the tailor, much disturbed.

"William," said the wife, "I am a mother, and a mother's heart can feel right; nature tells me that it is wrong for us to thrust out our children before they are old enough to go into the world. Let us keep them home longer."

"We cannot, and pay off this debt."

"Then let the debt go unpaid for the present. Those to whom it is owed can receive no harm from waiting; but our children will" —

Just then a man brought in a letter, and, handing it to the tailor, withdrew. On breaking the seal, Mr. Moale found that it contained fifty dollars, and read as follows:—

"SIR—Upon reflection, I feel that I ought not to receive from you the money that was due to me when you became unfortunate some years ago. I understand that you have a large family, that your health is not very good, and that you are depriving the one of comforts, and injuring the other, in endeavouring to pay off your old debts. To cancel these obligations would be all right—nay, your duty—if you could do so without neglecting higher and plainer duties. But you cannot do this, and I cannot receive the money you paid me this morning. Take it back, and let it be expended in making your family more comfortable. I have enough, and more than enough for all my wants, and I will not deprive you of a sum that must be important, while to me it is of little consequence either as gained or lost.

EDWARD PETRON."

The letter dropped from the tailor's hand; he was overcome with emotion. His wife, when she understood its purport, burst into tears.

The merchant's sleep was sweeter that night than it had been for some time, and so was the sleep of the poor debtor.

The next day Mr. Moale called to see Mr. Petron, to whom, at the instance of the latter, he gave a full detail of his actual circumstances. The merchant was touched by his story, and prompted by true benevolence to aid him in his struggles. He saw most of the tailor's old creditors, and induced those who had not been paid in full to voluntarily relinquish their claims, and some of those who had received money since the poor man's misfortunes, to restore it as belonging of right to his family. There was not one of these creditors who did not feel happier by their act of generosity; and no one can doubt that both the tailor and his family were also happier. John and Henry were not compelled to leave their home until they were older and better prepared to endure the privations that usually attend the boy's first entrance into the world; and help for the mother in her arduous duties could now be afforded.

No one doubts that the creditor, whose money is not paid to him, has rights. But too few think of the rights of the poor debtor, who sinks into obscurity, and often privations, while his heart is oppressed with a sense of obligations utterly beyond his power to cancel.

THE SUNDAY CHRISTIAN.

TWO things are required to make a Christian—piety and charity. The first has relation to worship, and in the last all social duties are involved. Of the great importance of charity in the Christian character, some idea may be gained by the pointed question asked by an apostle—"If you love not your brother whom you have seen, how can you love God whom you have not seen?" There is no mistaking the meaning of this. It says, in the plainest language—"Piety without charity is nothing;" and yet how many thousands and hundreds of thousands around us expect to get to heaven by Sunday religion alone! Through the week they reach out their hands for money on the right and on the left, so eager for its attainment, that little or no regard is paid to the interests of others; and on Sunday, with a pious face, they attend church and enter into the most holy acts of worship, fondly imagining that they can be saved by mere acts of piety, while no regard for their fellow-man is in their hearts.

Such a man was Brian Rowley. His religion was of so pure a stamp that it would not bear the world's rough contact, and, therefore, it was never brought into the world. He left the world to take care of itself when the Sabbath morning broke; and when the Sabbath morning closed, he went back into the world to look after his own interests. Every Sunday he progressed a certain way towards heaven, and then stood still for a week, in order that he might take proper care of the dollars and cents.

Business men who had transactions with Mr. Rowley generally kept their eyes open. If they did not do it at the first operation, they rarely omitted it afterwards, and for sufficient reason; he was sharp at making a bargain, and never felt satisfied unless he obtained some advantage. Men engaged in mercantile pursuits were looked upon, as a general thing, as ungodly in their lives, and therefore, in a certain sense, "out-siders." To make good bargains out of these was only to fight them with their own weapons; and he was certainly good at such work. In dealing with his brethren of the same faith he was rather more guarded, and affected a contempt for carnal things that he did not feel.

We said that the religion of Mr. Rowley did not go beyond the pious duties of the Sabbath. This must be amended. His piety flowed into certain benevolent operations of the day; he contributed to the support of Indian and Foreign Missions, and was one of the managers on a Tract Board. In the affairs of the Ceylonese and South-Sea Islanders he took a warm interest, and could talk eloquently about the heathen.

Not far from Mr. Brian Rowley's place of business was the store of a man named Lane, whose character had been cast originally in a different mould. He was not a church-going man, because, as he said, he didn't want to be "thought a hypocrite." In this he displayed a weakness. At one time he owned a pew in the same church to which Rowley was attached, and attended church regularly, although he did not attach himself to the church, nor receive its ordinances. His pew was near that of Mr. Rowley, and he had a good opportunity for observing the peculiar manner in which the latter performed his devotions. Unfortunately for his good opinion of the pious Sunday worshipper, they were brought into rather close contact during the week in matters of business, when Mr. Lane had opportunities of contrasting his piety and charity. The want of agreement in these two pre-requisites of a genuine Christian disgusted Lane, and caused him so much annoyance on Sunday that he finally determined to give up his pew and remain at home. A disposition to carp at professors of religion was manifested from this time; the whole were judged by Rowley as a sample.

One dull day a man named Gregory, a sort of busybody in the neighbourhood, came into the store of Mr. Lane and said to him— "What do you think of our friend Rowley? Is he a good Christian?"

"He's a pretty fair Sunday Christian," replied Lane.

"What is that?" asked the man.

"A hypocrite, to use plain language."

"That's pretty hard talk," said Gregory.

"Do you think so?"

"Yes. When you call a man a hypocrite, you make him out, in my opinion, about as bad as he can well be."

"Call him a Sunday Christian, then."

"A Sunday Christian?"

"Yes; that is, a man who puts his religion on every Sabbath, as he does his Sunday coat; and lays it away again carefully on Monday morning, so that it will receive no injury in every-day contact with the world."

"I believe with you that Rowley doesn't bring much of his religion into his business."

"No, nor as much common honesty as would save him from perdition."

"He doesn't expect to be saved by keeping the moral law."

"There'll be a poor chance for him, in my opinion, if he's judged finally by that code."

"You don't seem to have a very high opinion of our friend Rowley?"

"I own that. I used to go to church; but his pious face was ever before me, and his psalm-singing ever in my ears. Was it possible to look at him and not think of his grasping, selfish, overreaching conduct in all his business transactions through the week? No, it was not possible for me. And so, in disgust, I gave up my pew, and haven't been to church since."

The next man whom Gregory met he made the repository of what Lane had said about Rowley. This person happened to be a member of the church, and felt scandalized by the remarks. After a little reflection he concluded to inform Mr. Rowley of the free manner in which Mr. Lane had spoken of him.

"Called me a hypocrite!" exclaimed the indignant Mr. Rowley, as soon as he was advised of the free manner in which Mr. Lane had talked about him.

"So I understand. Gregory was my informant."

Mr. Gregory was called upon, and confirmed the statement. Rowley was highly indignant, and while the heat of his anger was upon him, called at the store of Mr. Lane, in company with two members of his church, who were not at all familiar with his business character, and, therefore, held him in pretty high estimation as a man of piety and sincerity.

The moment Mr. Lane saw these three men enter his place of business, he had a suspicion of their errand.

"Can I have some private conversation with you?" asked Mr. Rowley, with a countenance as solemn as the grave.

"Certainly," replied Mr. Lane, not the least discomposed. "Walk back into my counting-room. We shall be entirely alone there. Do you wish your friends present?"

"I do," was gravely replied; "I brought them for that purpose."

"Walk back, gentlemen," said Lane, as he turned to lead the way.

The four men retired to the little office of the merchant in the back part of the store. After they were seated, Lane said:

"Well, Mr. Rowley, I am ready to hear what you have to say."

Mr. Rowley cleared his throat two or three times, and then said, in a voice that indicated a good deal of inward disturbance:

"I understand that you have been making rather free use of my name of late."

"Indeed! in what way?" Lane was perfectly self-possessed.

"I am told that you went so far as to call me a hypocrite." The voice of Rowley trembled.

"I said you were a Sunday Christian," replied Lane.

"What do you mean by that?" was peremptorily demanded.

"A man whose religion is a Sunday affair altogether. One who expects to get to heaven by pious observances and church-goings on the Sabbath, without being over-particular as to the morality of his conduct through the week."

"Morality! do you pretend to say that I am an immoral man?" said Rowley, with much heat.

"Don't get into a passion!" returned Lane, coolly. "That will not help us at all in this grave matter."

Rowley quivered in every nerve; but the presence of his two brethren admonished him that a Christian temper was very necessary to be maintained on the occasion.

"Do you charge me with want of morality?" he said, with less visible excitement.

"I do,—that is, according to my code of morality."

"Upon what do you base your code?" asked one of the witnesses of this rather strange interview.

"On the Bible," replied Lane.

"Indeed!" was answered, with some surprise; "on what part of it?"

"On every part. But more particularly that passage in the New Testament where the whole of the law and the prophets is condensed in a single passage, enjoining love to our neighbour as well as God."

Rowley and his friends looked surprised at this remark.

"Explain yourself," said the former, with a knit brow.

"That is easily done. The precept here given, and it comes from the highest authority, expressly declares, as I understand it, religion to consist in acting justly toward all men, as well as in pious acts towards God. If a man love not his brother whom he hath seen, how can he love God whom he hath not seen?"

"Does our brother Rowley deny that?" asked the men present.

"If a man's life is any index to his faith, I would say that he does," replied Mr. Lane.

A deep crimson overspread the face of Mr. Rowley.

"I didn't expect insult when I came here," said he in a trembling voice.

"Nor have I offered any," replied Mr. Lane.

"You have thought proper to ask me a number of very pointed questions, and I have merely answered them according to my views of truth."

"You make a very sweeping declaration," said one of the friends of Rowley. "Suppose you give some proof of your assertion?"

"That I can readily do if it is desired."

"I desire it, then," said Rowley.

"Do you remember the five bales of cotton you sold to Peterson?" inquired Mr. Lane.

Rowley replied that he did, but evinced some uneasiness of manner at the question.

"They were damaged," said Lane.

"I sold them as I bought them," returned Rowley.

"Did you buy them as damaged?"

"No, I bought the cotton as a good article."

"And sold it as good?"

Mr. Rowley seemed a little confused.

"I sold the cotton at twelve cents a pound," was the reply. "Nothing was said about the quality."

"Twelve cents is the price of a prime article. If you had been asked by Peterson if the cotton were in good condition, would you have answered affirmatively?"

"Do you think I would tell a lie?" asked Mr. Rowley, indignantly.

"Our acts are the most perfect expressions of our intentions," replied Mr. Lane. "You were deceived in your purchase of the cotton; the article proved so near valueless, as not to be really worth three cents a pound. You discovered this, as I have the best reasons for knowing, almost as soon as it came into your possession; and yet you offered it to Peterson, who, not suspecting for a moment that any thing was wrong, bought it at the regular market-rate as good. You saved yourself; but Peterson, though not a professor of religion, was too honest to put his bad bargain off upon another. Now, if that act, on your part, was loving your neighbour as yourself, I must own to a very perverted understanding of the sacred precept. I, though no church member, would have put my head into the fire rather than do such an act."

Mr. Rowley, much confused by so direct a charge, attempted to explain the matter away, alleging that he did not think that the article was so badly damaged—that he sold as he bought—that it wasn't right that he should bear all the loss, with much more to the same purpose; to all of which Lane opposed but little. He had presented the case already strong enough for all to see how far it comported with Christian morality. But he had more to say:—

"Beyond this, which I bring forward as a specimen of the character of your dealings with your fellow-men, I could adduce almost innumerable examples of your indirect and covert modes of obtaining the advantage in ordinary transactions. You may not be aware of the fact, Mr. Rowley, but your reputation among business men is that of a dealer so close to your own side of the bargain as to trench upon the rights of others. You invariably keep the half cent in giving change, while you have been repeatedly known to refuse a ten cent piece and two cents for an elevenpence. In fact, you are known as a man who invariably seeks to get the best of every transaction. If this is Christian charity—if this is a just regard for the rights of your neighbours—if this is in agreement with the spirit of the Bible, then I have been labouring under a mental delusion. Man of the world as I am—heathen as you have seemed to regard me, I am proud to say that I govern my actions from a higher principle. You now understand, gentlemen," addressing the friends of Rowley, "why I have called this man a Sunday Christian. It is plain that he expects to get to heaven by a simple Sunday service of his Maker, while all the week he pursues gain so eagerly as to thrust other people aside, and even make his way, so to speak, over their prostrate bodies. I have no more to say."

Rowley was so much confounded by this unexpected charge, that he was silent. His own conscience wrote an affirmation of the truth in his countenance. The men who had come with him arose, and, bowing with far more respect than when they entered, withdrew, and Rowley went with them.

There was a change in the pious merchant after this. He conducted his business with less apparent eagerness to get the best of every bargain than had been his custom in former times; but whether influenced by more genuine Christian principles, or by an awakened love of reputation, it is not for us to say.

It is not by a man's religious profession that the world judges of his character, but by the quality of his transactions in business intercourse with his fellow-men. If he be truly religious, it will be seen here in the justice and judgment of all his business transactions. If a man be not faithful to his brother, he cannot be faithful to Heaven.

I KNEW HOW IT WOULD BE.

"HE'LL never succeed!" was the remark of Mr. Hueston, on reference being made to a young man named Eldridge, who had recently commenced business.

"Why not?" was asked.

"He's begun wrong."

"In what way?"

"His connection is bad."

"With Dalton?"

"Yes. Dalton is either a knave or a fool. The former, I believe; but in either case the result will be the same to his partner. Before two years, unless a miracle takes place, you will see Eldridge, at least, coming out at the little end of the horn. I could have told him this at first, but it was none of my business. I never meddle with things that don't concern me."

"You know Dalton, then?"

"I think I do."

"Has he been in business before?"

"Yes, half a dozen times; and somehow or other, he has always managed to get out of it, with cash in hand, long enough before it broke down to escape all odium and responsibility."

"I'm sorry for Eldridge. He's a clever young man, and honest into the bargain."

"Yes; and he has energy of character and some business talents. But he is too confiding. And here is just the weakness that will prove his ruin. He will put too much faith in his plausible associate."

"Some one should warn him of his danger. Were I intimate enough to venture on the freedom, I would certainly do so."

"I don't meddle myself with other people's affairs. One never gets any thanks for the trouble he takes on this score. At least, that is my experience. And, moreover, it's about as much as I can do to take good care of my own concerns. This is every man's business."

"I wish you had given the young man a word of caution before he was involved with Dalton."

"I did think of doing so; but then I reflected that it was his look-out, and not mine. Each man has to cut his eye-teeth for himself, you know."

"True; but when we see a stumbling-block in the way of a blind man, or one whose eyes are turned in another direction, we ought at least to utter a warning word. It seems to me that we owe that much good-will to our fellows."

"Perhaps we do. And I don't know that it would have been any harm if I had done as you suggest. However, it is too late now."

"I think not. A hint of the truth would put him on his guard."

"I don't know."

"Oh, yes, it would."

"I am not certain. Dalton is a most plausible man; and I am pretty sure that, in the mind of a person like Eldridge, he can inspire the fullest confidence. To suggest any thing wrong, now, would not put him on his guard, and might lead the suggester into trouble."

Much more was said on both sides, but no good result flowed from the conversation. Mr. Hueston did not hesitate to declare that he knew how it would all be in the end; but at the same time said that it was none of his business, and that "every man must look out for himself."

The character of Dalton was by no means harshly judged by Mr. Hueston. He was, at heart, a knave; yet a most cunning and specious one. Eldridge, on the contrary, was the very soul of integrity; and, being thoroughly honest in all his intentions, it was hard for him to believe that any man who spoke fair to him, and professed to be governed by right principles, could be a scoundrel. With a few thousand dollars, his share of his father's estate, he had come to Boston for the purpose of commencing some kind of business. With creditable prudence, he entered the store of a merchant and remained there for a year, in order to obtain a practical familiarity with trade. During this period he fell in with Dalton, who was in a small commission way that barely yielded him enough to meet his expenses. Dalton was not long in discovering that Eldridge had some cash, and that his ultimate intention was to engage in business for himself. From that time he evinced towards the young man a very friendly spirit, and soon found a good reason for changing his boarding-place, and making his home under the same roof with Eldridge. To win upon the young man's confidence was no hard matter. Before six months, Dalton was looked upon as a generous-minded friend, who had his interest deeply at heart. All his views in regard to business were freely communicated; and he rested upon the suggestions of Dalton with the confidence of one who believed that he had met a friend, not only fully competent to advise aright, but thoroughly unselfish in all his feelings.

Dalton possessed a large amount of business information, and was, therefore, the very man for Eldridge; particularly as he was communicative. In conversation, the latter obtained a great deal of information on subjects especially interesting to one who looked forward to engaging in some branch of trade for himself. One evening the two men sat conversing about business, as usual, when Eldridge said:

"It is time I was making some move for myself; but, for my life, I can't come to any decision as to what I shall do."

"It is better for a young man, if he can do so, to connect himself with some established house," replied Dalton to this. "It takes time to make a new business, and not unfrequently a very long time."

"I am aware of that; but I see no opportunity for an arrangement of the kind."

"How much capital can you furnish?"

"Ten thousand dollars."

"That's very good, and ought to enable you to make an arrangement somewhere. I don't know but I might be willing to give you an interest in my business. This, however, would require some reflection. I am turning out a very handsome surplus every year, without at all crowding sail."

"A commission business?"

"Yes. I am agent for three or four manufactories, and effect some pretty large sales during the year. If I were able to make liberal cash advances, I could more than quadruple my business."

"And, of course, your profits also?"

"Yes, that follows as a natural result."

"Would ten thousand dollars be at all adequate for such a purpose?"

"It would help very much. Ten thousand dollars in cash is, you know, a basis of credit to nearly four times that sum."

"Yes, I am aware of that."

"Is your capital readily available?" inquired Dalton.

"Yes, since I have been in the city I have invested every thing in government securities, as safe property, and readily convertible into cash."

"Very judicious."

Dalton mused for some time.

"Yes," he at length said, as if he had been thinking seriously of the effect of ten thousand dollars in his business. "The capital you have would put a new face on every thing. That's certain. Suppose you think the matter over, and I will do the same."

"I will, certainly. And I may say now, that there will hardly be any hinderance on my part to the arrangement, if you should see it to be advantageous all around."

Of course Mr. Dalton professed, after taking a decent time for pretended reflection, to see great advantage to all parties in a business connection, which in due time was formed. But few of those who knew Eldridge were apprized of what he intended doing, and those who did know, and were aware at the same time of Mr. Dalton's character, like Mr. Hueston, concluded to mind their own business.

And so, unwarned of the risk he was encountering, an honest and confiding young man was permitted to form a copartnership with a villain, who had already been the means of involving three or four unsuspecting individuals in hopeless embarrassment.

Confident that he had entered the road to fortune, Eldridge commenced his new career. The capital he had supplied gave, as Dalton had predicted, new life to the business, for the offer of liberal cash advances brought heavier consignments, and opened the way for more extensive operations. The general management of affairs was left, according to previous understanding, in the hands of the senior partner, as most competent for that department; while Eldridge gave his mind to the practical details of the business, which, by the end of a year, had grown far beyond his anticipations.

Accepting large consignments of goods, upon which advances had to be made, required the raising of a great deal of money; and this Dalton managed to accomplish without calling away the attention of his partner from what he was engaged in doing. Thus matters went on for about three years, when Dalton began to complain of failing health, and to hint that he would be compelled to retire from active business. Eldridge said that he must not think of this; but the senior partner did think of it very seriously. From that time his health appeared to break rapidly; and in a few months he formally announced his intention to withdraw. Finding both remonstrance and persuasion of no avail, the basis of a dissolution of the copartnership was agreed upon, in which the value of the business itself, that would now be entirely in the hands of Eldridge, was rated high as an offset to a pretty large sum which Dalton claimed as his share in the concern. Without due reflection, there being a balance of five thousand dollars to the credit of the firm in bank, which, by the way, was provided for special effect at the time by the cunning senior, Eldridge consented that, for his share of the business, Dalton should be permitted to take bills receivable amounting to six thousand dollars; a check for two thousand, and his notes for ten thousand dollars besides, payable in three to eighteen months. After all this was settled, a dissolution of the copartnership was publicly announced, and Eldridge, with some misgivings at heart, undertook the entire management of the business himself. It was but a very little while before he found himself embarrassed in making his payments. The withdrawal of two thousand dollars in cash, and six thousand in paper convertible into cash, created a serious disability. In fact, an earnest and thorough investigation of the whole business showed it to be so crippled that little less than a miracle would enable him to conduct it to a safe issue. Nevertheless, still unsuspicious to the real truth, he resolved to struggle manfully for a triumph over the difficulties that lay before him, and overcome them, if there was any virtue in energy and perseverance.

The first point at which the business suffered was in the loss of consignments. Inability to make the required advances turned from the warehouse of Eldridge large lots of goods almost weekly, the profits on the sales of which would have been a handsome addition to his income. At the end of three months, the first note of a thousand dollars held by Dalton fell due, and was paid. This was so much more taken from his capital. Another month brought a payment of a like amount, and at the end of six months a thousand dollars more were paid. Thus Dalton had been able to get eleven thousand dollars out of the concern, although three years before he was not really worth a dollar; and there were still due him seven thousand dollars.

By this time, the eyes of Eldridge were beginning to open to the truth. Suspicion being once finally awakened, he entered upon a careful examination of the business from the time of forming the copartnership. This occupied him for some weeks before he was able to bring out a clear and comprehensive exhibit of affairs. Then he saw that he had been the victim of a specious and cunning scoundrel, and that, so far from being worth a dollar, he had obligations falling due for over ten thousand dollars more than he had the means to pay.

A sad and disheartening result! And what added to the pain of Eldridge was the fact, that he should have been so weak and short-sighted as to permit himself to be thus duped and cheated.

"I knew how it would be," said Mr. Hueston, coolly, when he was told that Eldridge was in difficulties. "Nothing else was to have been expected."

"Why so?" inquired the person to whom the remark was made.

"Everybody knows Dalton to be a sharper. Eldridge is not his first victim."

"I did not know it."

"I did, then, and prophesied just this result."

"You?"

"Yes, certainly I did. I knew exactly how it must turn out. And here's the end, as I predicted."

This was said with great self-complacency.

Soon after the conversation, a young man, named Williams, who had only a year before married the daughter of Mr. Hueston, came into his store with a look of trouble on his countenance. His business was that of an exchange-broker, and in conducting it he was using the credit of his father-in-law quite liberally.

"What's the matter?" inquired Mr. Hueston, seeing, by the expression of the young man's face, that something was wrong.

"Have you heard any thing about Eldridge?" inquired Williams, in an anxious voice.

"Yes, I understand that he is about making a failure of it; and, if so, it will be a bad one. But what has that to do with your affairs?"

"If he fails, I am ruined," replied the young man, becoming greatly excited.

"You?" It was now Mr. Hueston's turn to exhibit a disturbed aspect.

"I hold seven thousand dollars of his paper."

"Seven thousand dollars!"

"Yes."

"How in the name of wonder did it come into your possession?"

"I took it from Dalton at a tempting discount."

"From Dalton! Then his name is on the paper?"

"No, I hold it without recourse."

"What folly! How could you have done such a thing?"

"I believed Eldridge to be perfectly good. Dalton said that he was in the way of making a fortune."

"Why, then, was he anxious to part with his paper without recourse?"

"It was, he alleged, on account of ill-health. He wished to close up all his business and make an investment of what little he possessed previous to going south, in the hope that a change of air would brace up his shattered constitution."

"It was all a lie—the scoundrel! His health is as good as mine. A greater villain than he is does not walk the earth. I wonder how you could have been so duped."

"How do you think Eldridge's affairs will turn out?" asked the young man.

"Worse than nothing, I suppose. I understand that he paid Dalton some eighteen thousand dollars for his half of the business. There was but ten thousand dollars capital at first; and, from the way things were conducted, instead of its increasing, it must have diminished yearly."

Here was an entirely new aspect in the case. Mr. Hueston's self-complacency was gone; he knew how it would be with Eldridge from the first, but he didn't know how it was going to be with himself. He didn't for a moment dream that when the fabric of the young man's fortune came falling around him, that any thing belonging to him would be buried under the ruins.

"Too bad! too bad!" he ejaculated, as, under a sense of the utter desperation of the case, he struck his hands together, and then threw them above his head. But it did no good to fret and scold, and blame his son-in-law; the error had been committed, and it was now too late to retrace a step. Six or seven thousand dollars would inevitably be lost; and, as Williams had no capital, originally, of his own, the money would have to come out of his pocket. The ruin of which the young man talked was more in his imagination than anywhere else, as Mr. Hueston was able enough to sustain him in his difficulty.

In the winding up of the affairs of Eldridge, who stopped payment on the day Williams announced to his father-in-law the fact that he held his notes, every thing turned out as badly as Mr. Hueston had predicted. The unhappy young man was almost beside himself with trouble, mortification, and disappointment. Not only had he lost every thing he possessed in the world; he was deeply involved in debt besides, and his good name was gone. A marriage contract, into which he had entered, was broken off in consequence; the father of the lady demanding of him a release of the engagement in a way so insulting, that the young man flung insult back into his teeth, and never after went near his house.

For months after the disastrous termination of his business, Eldridge lingered about the city in a miserable state of mind. Some friends obtained for him a situation as clerk, but he did not keep the place very long; it seemed almost impossible for him to fix his attention upon any thing. This neglect of the interests of his employer was so apparent, that he was dismissed from his place at the end of a few months. This increased the morbid despondency under which he was labouring, and led to an almost total abandonment of himself. In less than a year, he was travelling swiftly along the road to utter ruin.

One day, it was just twelve months from the time of Eldridge's failure, Mr. Hueston stood conversing with a gentleman, when the unhappy young man went reeling by, so much intoxicated that he with difficulty kept his feet.

"Poor fellow!" said the gentleman, in a tone of pity. "He was badly dealt by."

"There is no doubt of that," returned Mr. Hueston. "Dalton managed his cards with his usual skill. But I knew how it would be from the first. I knew that Dalton was a knave at heart, and would overreach him."

"You did?" was rejoined, with a look and tone of surprise.

"Oh, yes. I predicted, from the beginning, the very result that has come out."

"You warned the young man, of course?" inquired the gentleman.

"No."

"What! Saw him in the hands of a sharper, and gave him no warning?"

"I never meddle in other people's affairs. I find as much as I can do to take proper care of my own."

"And yet, if common report is true, had you taken a little care of this young man, you would have saved six or seven thousand dollars for yourself."

"That's my look-out," said Mr. Hueston.

"You knew how it would be," resumed the gentleman, in a severe, rebuking voice, "and yet kept silence, permitting an honest, confiding young man to fall into the clutches of a scoundrel. Mr. Hueston, society holds you responsible for the ruin of one of its members, equally responsible with the knave who was the agent of the ruin. A word would have saved the young man; but, in your indifference and disregard of others' good, you would not speak that word. When next you see the miserable wreck of a human being that but just now went staggering past, remember the work of your own hands is before you."

And saying this, the man turned abruptly away, leaving Mr. Hueston so much astonished and bewildered by the unexpected charge, as scarcely to comprehend where he was. Recovering himself in a moment or two, he walked slowly along, his eyes upon the ground, with what feelings the reader may imagine.

A few days afterwards, his son-in-law, at his instance, went in search of Eldridge for the purpose of offering him assistance, and making an effort to reclaim him. But, alas! he was too late; death had finished the work of ruin.

Words for the Wise

JACOB JONES;

OR, THE MAN WHO COULDN'T GET ALONG IN THE WORLD.

JACOB JONES was clerk in a commission store at a salary of five hundred dollars a year. He was just twenty-two, and had been receiving his salary for two years. Jacob had no one to care for but himself; but, somehow or other, it happened that he did not lay up any money, but, instead, usually had from fifty to one hundred dollars standing against him on the books of his tailors.

"How much money have you laid by, Jacob?" said, one day, the merchant who employed him. This question came upon Jacob rather suddenly; and coming from the source that it did was not an agreeable one—for the merchant was a very careful and economical man.

"I haven't laid by any thing yet," replied Jacob, with a slight air of embarrassment.

"You haven't!" said the merchant, in surprise. "Why, what have you done with your money?"

"I've spent it, somehow or other."

"It must have been somehow or other. I should think, or somehow else," returned the employer, half seriously, and half playfully. "But really, Jacob, you are a very thoughtless young man to waste your money."

"I don't think I *waste* my money," said Jacob.

"What, then, have you done with it?" asked the merchant.

"It costs me the whole amount of my salary to live."

The merchant shook his head.

"Then you live extravagantly for a young man of your age and condition. How much do you pay for boarding?"

"Four dollars a week."

27

"Too much by from fifty cents to a dollar. But even paying that sum, four more dollars per week ought to meet fully all your other expenses, and leave you what would amount to nearly one hundred dollars per annum to lay by. I saved nearly two hundred dollars a year on a salary no larger than you receive."

"I should like very much to know how you did it. I can't save a cent; in fact, I hardly ever have ten dollars in my pocket."

"Where does your money go, Jacob? In what way do you spend a hundred dollars a year more than is necessary?"

"It is spent, I know; and that is pretty much all I can tell about it," replied Jacob.

"You can certainly tell by your private account-book."

"I don't keep any private account, sir."

"You don't?" in surprise.

"No, sir. What's the use? My salary is five hundred dollars a year, and wouldn't be any more nor less if I kept an account of every half cent of it."

"Humph!"

The merchant said no more. His mind was made up about his clerk. The fact that he spent five hundred dollars a year, and kept no private account, was enough for him.

"He'll never be any good to himself nor anybody else. Spend his whole salary—humph! Keep no private account—humph!"

This was the opinion held of Jacob Jones by his employer from that day. The reason why he had inquired as to how much money he had saved was this. He had a nephew, a poor young man, who, like Jacob, was a clerk, and showed a good deal of ability for business. His salary was rather more than what Jacob received, and, like Jacob, he spent it all; but not on himself. He supported, mainly, his mother and a younger brother and sister. A good chance for a small, but safe beginning, was seen by the uncle, which would require only about a thousand dollars as an investment. In his opinion it would be just the thing for Jacob and the nephew. Supposing that Jacob had four or five hundred dollars laid by, it was his intention, if he approved of the thing, to furnish his nephew with a like sum, in order to join him and to enter into business. But the acknowledgment of Jacob that he had not saved a dollar, and that he kept no private account, settled the matter in the merchant's mind, as far as he was concerned.

About a month afterward, Jacob met his employer's nephew, who said,

"I am going into business."

"You are?"

"Yes."

"What are you going to do?"

"Open a commission store."

"Ah! Can you get any good consignments?"

"I am to have the agency for a new mill, which has just commenced operations, besides consignments of goods from several small concerns at the East."

"You will have to make advances."

"To no great extent. My uncle has secured the agency of the new mill here without any advance being required, and eight hundred or a thousand dollars will be as much as I shall need to secure as many goods as I can sell from the other establishments of which I speak."

"But where will the eight hundred or a thousand dollars come from?"

"My uncle has placed a thousand dollars at my disposal. Indeed, the whole thing is the result of his recommendation."

"Your uncle! You are a lucky dog. I wish I had a rich uncle. But there is no such good fortune for me."

This was the conclusion of Jacob Jones, who made himself quite unhappy for some weeks, brooding over the matter. He never once dreamed of the real cause of his not having had an equal share in his young friend's good fortune. He had not the most distant idea that his employer felt nearly as much regard for him as for his nephew, and would have promoted his interests as quickly, if he had felt justified in doing so.

"It's my luck, I suppose," was the final conclusion of his mind; "and it's no use to cry about it. Anyhow, it isn't every man with a rich uncle, and a thousand dollars advanced, who succeeds in business, nor every man who starts without capital that is unsuccessful. I understand as much about business as the old man's nephew, any day; and can get consignments as well as he can."

Three or four months after this, Jacob notified the merchant that he was going to start for himself, and asked his interest as far as he could give it, without interfering with his own business. His employer did not speak very encouragingly about the matter, which offended Jacob.

"He's afraid I'll injure his nephew," said he to himself. "But he needn't be uneasy—the world is wide enough for us all, the old hunks!"

Jacob borrowed a couple of hundred dollars, took a store at five hundred dollars a year rent, and employed a clerk and porter. He then sent his circulars to a number of manufactories at the East, announcing the fact of his having opened a new commission house, and soliciting consignments. His next move was, to leave his boarding-house, where he had been paying four dollars a week, and take lodgings at a hotel at seven dollars a week.

Notwithstanding Jacob went regularly to the post-office twice every day, few letters came to hand, and but few of them contained bills of lading and invoices. The result of the first year's business was an income from commission on sales of seven hundred dollars. Against this were the items of one thousand dollars for personal expenses, five hundred dollars for store-rent, seven hundred dollars for clerk and porter, and for petty and contingent expenses two hundred dollars; leaving the uncomfortable deficit of seventeen hundred dollars, which stood against him in the form of bills payable for sales effected, and small notes of accommodation borrowed from his friends.

The result of the first year's business of his old employer's nephew was very different. The gross profits were three thousand dollars, and the expenses as follows: personal expense, seven hundred dollars—just what the young man's salary had previously been, and out of which he supported his mother and her family—store rent, three hundred dollars; porter, two hundred and fifty; petty expenses, one hundred dollars—in all thirteen hundred and fifty dollars, leaving a net profit of sixteen hundred and fifty dollars. It will be seen that he did not go to the expense of a clerk during the first year. He preferred working a little harder, and keeping his own books, by which an important saving was effected.

At the end of the second year, notwithstanding Jacob Jones's business more than doubled itself, he was compelled to wind up, and found himself twenty-five hundred dollars worse than nothing. Several of his unpaid bills to eastern houses were placed in suit, and as he lived in a state where imprisonment for debt still existed, he was compelled to go through the forms required by the insolvent laws, to keep clear of durance vile.

At the very period when he was driven under by adverse gales, his young friend, who had gone into business about the same time, found himself under the necessity of employing a clerk. He offered Jones a salary of four hundred dollars, the most he believed himself yet justified in paying. This was accepted, and Jacob found himself once more standing upon *terra firma*, although the portion upon which his feet rested was very small; still it was *terra firma*—and that was something.

The real causes of his ill success never for a moment occurred to the mind of Jacob. He considered himself an "unlucky dog."

"Every thing that some people touch turns into money," he would sometimes say. "But I was not born under a lucky star."

Instead of rigidly bringing down his expenses, as he ought to have done, to four hundred dollars, if he had to live in a garret and cook his own food, Jacob went back to his old boarding-house, and paid four dollars a week. All his other expenses required at least eight dollars more to meet them. He was perfectly aware that he was living beyond his income—the exact excess he did not stop to ascertain—but he expected an increase of salary before long, as a matter of course, either in his present situation or in a new one. But no increase took place for two years, and then he was between three and four hundred dollars in debt to tailors, boot-makers, his landlady, and to sundry friends, to whom he applied for small sums of money in cases of emergency.

One day, about this time, two men were conversing together quite earnestly, as they walked leisurely along one of the principal streets of the city where Jacob resided. One was past the prime of life, and the other about twenty-two. They were father and son, and the subject of conversation related to the wish of the latter to enter into business. The father did not think the young man was possessed of sufficient knowledge of business or experience, and was, therefore, desirous of associating some one with him who could make up these deficiencies. If he could find just the person that pleased him, he was ready to advance capital and credit to an amount somewhere within the neighbourhood of twenty thousand dollars. For some months he had been thinking of Jacob, who was a first-rate salesman, had a good address, and was believed by him to possess business habits eminently conducive to success. The fact that he had once failed was something of a drawback in his mind, but he had asked Jacob the reason of his ill-success, which was so plausibly explained, that he considered the young man as simply unfortunate in not having capital, and nothing else.

"I think Mr. Jones just the right man for you," said the father, as they walked along.

"I don't know of any one with whom I had rather form a business connection. He is a man of good address, business habits, and, as far as I know, good principles."

"Suppose you mention the subject to him this afternoon."

This was agreed to. The two men then entered the shop of a fashionable tailor, for the purpose of ordering some clothes. While there, a man having the appearance of a collector came in, and drew the tailor aside. The conversation was brief but earnest, and concluded by the tailor's saying, so loud that he could be heard by all who were standing near,

"It's no use to waste your time with him any longer. Just hand over the account to Simpson, and let him take care of it."

The collector turned away, and the tailor came back to his customers.

"It is too bad," said he, "the way some of these young fellows do serve us. I have now several thousand dollars on my books against clerks who receive salaries large enough to support them handsomely, and I can't collect a dollar of it. There is Jacob Jones, whose account I have just ordered to be placed in the hands of a lawyer, he owes me nearly two hundred dollars, and I can't get a cent out of him. I call him little better than a scamp."

The father and son exchanged glances of significance, but said nothing. The fate of Jacob Jones was sealed.

"If that is the case," said the father, as they stepped into the street, "the less we have to do with him the better."

To this the son assented. Another more prudent young man was selected, whose fortune was made.

When Jacob received Lawyer Simpson's note, threatening a suit if the tailor's bill was not paid, he was greatly disturbed.

"Am I not the most unfortunate man in the world?" said he to himself, by way of consolation. "After having paid him so much money, to be served like this. It is too bad. But this is the way of the world. Let a poor devil once get a little under the weather, every one must have a kick at him."

In this dilemma poor Jacob had to call upon the tailor, and beg him for further time. This was humiliating, especially as the tailor was considerably out of humour, and disposed to be hard with him. A threat to apply for the benefit of the insolvent law again, if a suit was pressed to an issue, finally induced the tailor to waive legal proceedings for the present, and Jacob had the immediate terrors of the law taken from before his eyes.

This event set Jacob to thinking and calculating, which he had never before deemed necessary in his private affairs. The result did not make him feel any happier. To his astonishment, he ascertained that he owed more than the whole of his next year's salary would pay, while that was not in itself sufficient to meet his current expenses.

For some weeks after this discovery of the real state of his affairs, Jacob was very unhappy. He applied for an increase of salary, and obtained one hundred dollars per annum. This was something, which was about all that could be said. If he could live on four hundred dollars a year, which he had never yet been able to do, the addition to his salary would not pay his tailor's bill within two years; and what was he to do with boot-maker, landlady, and others?

It happened about this time that a clerk in the bank where his old employer was director died. His salary was one thousand dollars. For the vacant place Jacob made immediate application, and was so fortunate as to secure it.

Under other circumstances, Jacob would have refused a salary of fifteen hundred dollars in a bank against five hundred in a counting-room, and for the reason that a bank-clerk has little or no hope beyond his salary all his life, while a counting-house clerk, if he have any aptness for trade, stands a fair chance of getting into business sooner or later, and making his fortune as a merchant. But a debt of four hundred dollars hanging over his head was an argument in favour of a clerkship in the bank, at a salary of a thousand dollars a year, not to be resisted.

"I'll keep it until I get even with the world again," he consoled himself by saying, "and then I'll go back into a counting-room. I've an ambition above being a bank-clerk all my life."

Painful experience had made Jacob a little wiser.

For the first time in his life he commenced keeping an account of his personal expenses. This acted as a salutary check upon his bad habit of spending money for every little thing that happened to strike his fancy, and enabled him to clear off his whole debt within the first year. Unwisely, however, he had, during this time, promised to pay some old debts, from which the law had released him. The persons holding these claims, finding him in the receipt of a higher salary, made an appeal to his honour, which, like an honest but imprudent man, he responded to by a promise of payment as soon as it was in his power. But little time elapsed after these promises were made before he found himself in the hands of constables and magistrates, and was only saved from imprisonment by getting friends to go his bail for six and nine months. In order to secure them, he had to give an order in advance for his salary. To get these burdens off his shoulders, it took twelve months longer, and then he was nearly thirty years of age.

"Thirty years old!" said he to himself on his thirtieth birth-day. "Can it be possible? Long before this I ought to have been doing a flourishing business, and here I am, nothing but a bank-clerk, with the prospect of never rising a step higher as long as I live. I don't know how it is that some people get along so well in the world. I'm sure I am as industrious, and can do business as well as any man; but here I am still at the point from which I started twenty years ago. I can't understand it. I'm afraid there's more in luck than I'm willing to believe."

From this time Jacob set himself to work to obtain a situation in some store or counting-room, and finally, after looking about for nearly a year, was fortunate enough to obtain a good place, as bookkeeper and salesman, with a wholesale grocer and commission merchant. Seven hundred dollars was to be his salary. His friends called him a fool for giving up an easy place at one thousand dollars a year, for a hard one at seven hundred. But the act was a much wiser one than many others of his life.

Instead of saving money during the third year of his receipt of one thousand dollars, he spent the whole of his salary, without paying off a single old debt. His private account-keeping had continued through a year and a half. After that it was abandoned. Had it been continued, it might have saved him three or four hundred dollars, which were now all gone, and nothing to show for them. Poor Jacob! Experience did not make him much wiser.

Two years passed, and at least half a dozen young men, here and there around our friend Jacob, went into business, either as partners in some old houses or under the auspices of relatives or interested friends. But there appeared no opening for him.

He did not know, that, many times during that period, he had been the subject of conversation between parties, one or both of which were looking out for a man, of thorough business qualifications, against which capital would be placed; nor the fact, that either his first failure, his improvidence, or something else personal to himself, had caused him to be set aside for some other one not near so capable.

He was lamenting his ill-luck one day, when a young man with whom he was very well acquainted, and who was clerk in a neighbouring store, called in and said he wanted to have some talk with him about a matter of interest to both.

"First of all, Mr. Jones," said the young man, after they were alone, "how much capital could you raise by a strong effort?"

"I am sure I don't know," replied Jacob, not in a very cheerful tone. "I never was lucky in having friends ready to assist me."

"Well! perhaps there will be no need of that. You have had a good salary for four or five years; how much have you saved? Enough, probably, to answer every purpose—that is, if you are willing to join me in taking advantage of one of the best openings for business that has offered for a long time. I have a thousand dollars in the Savings Bank. You have as much, or more, I presume?"

"I am sorry to say I have not," was poor Jacob's reply, in a desponding voice. "I was unfortunate in business some years ago, and my old debts have drained away from me every dollar I could earn."

"Indeed! that is unfortunate. I was in hopes you could furnish a thousand dollars."

"I might borrow it, perhaps, if the chance is a very good one."

"Well, if you could do that, it would be as well, I suppose," returned the young man. "But you must see about it immediately. If you cannot join me at once, I must find one who will, for the chance is too good to be lost."

Jacob got a full statement of the business proposed, its nature and prospects, and then laid the matter before the three merchants with whom he had at different times lived in the capacity of clerk, and begged them to advance him the required capital. The subject was taken up by them and seriously considered. They all liked Jacob, and felt willing to promote his interests, but had little or no confidence in his ultimate success, on account of his want of economy in personal matters. It was very justly remarked by one of them, that this want of economy, and judicious use of money in personal matters, would go with him in business, and mar all his prospects. Still, as they had great confidence in the other man, they agreed to advance, jointly, the sum needed.

In the mean time, the young man who had made the proposition to Jacob, when he learned that he had once failed in business, was still in debt, and liable to have claims pushed against him, (this he inferred from Jacob's having stretched the truth, by saying that his old debts drained away from him every dollar, when the fact was he was freed from them by the provisions of the insolvent law of the State,) came to the conclusion that a business connection with him was a thing to be avoided rather than sought after. He accordingly turned his thoughts in another quarter, and when Jones called to inform him that he had raised the capital needed, he was coolly told that it was too late, he having an hour before closed a partnership arrangement with another person, under the belief that Jones could not advance the money required.

This was a bitter disappointment, and soured the mind of Jacob against his fellow man, and against the fates also, which he alleged were all combined against him. His own share in the matter was a thing undreamed of. He believed himself far better qualified for business than the one who had been preferred before him, and he had the thousand dollars to advance. It must be his luck that was against him, nothing else; he could come to no other conclusion. Other people could get along in the world, but he couldn't. That was the great mystery of his life.

For two years Jacob had been waiting to get married. He had not wished to take this step before entering into business, and having a fair prospect before him. But years were creeping on him apace, and the fair object of his affections seemed weary of delay.

"It's no use to wait any longer," said he, after this dashing of his cup to the earth. "Luck is against me. I shall never be any thing but a poor devil of a clerk. If Clara is willing to share my humble lot, we might as well be married first as last."

Clara was not unwilling, and Jacob Jones entered into the estate connubial, and took upon him the cares of a family, with a salary of seven hundred dollars a year, to sustain the new order of things. Instead of taking cheap boarding, or renting a couple of rooms, and commencing housekeeping in a small way, Jacob saw but one course before him, and that was to rent a genteel house, go in debt for genteel furniture, and keep two servants. Two years were the longest that he could bear up under this state of things, when he was sold out by the sheriff, and forced "to go through the mill again," as taking the benefit of the insolvent law was facetiously called in the State where he resided.

"Poor fellow! he has a hard time of it. I wonder why it is that he gets along so badly. He is an industrious man and regular in his habits. It is strange. But some men seem born to ill-luck."

So said some of his pitying friends. Others understood the matter better.

Ten years have passed, and Jacob is still a clerk, but not in a store. Hopeless of getting into business, he applied for a vacancy that occurred in an insurance company, and received the appointment, which he still holds at a salary of twelve hundred dollars a year. After being sold out three times by the sheriff, and having the deep mortification of seeing her husband brought down to the humiliating necessity of applying as often for the benefit of the insolvent law, Mrs. Jones took affairs, by consent of her husband, into her own hands, and managed them with such prudence and economy, that, notwithstanding they have five children, the expenses, all told, are not over eight hundred dollars a year, and half of the surplus, four hundred dollars, is appropriated to the liquidation of debts contracted since their marriage, and the other half deposited in the Savings Bank, as a fund for the education of their children in the higher branches, when they reach a more advanced age.

To this day it is a matter of wonder to Jacob Jones why he could never get along in the world like some people; and he has come to the settled conviction that it is his "luck."

STARTING A NEWSPAPER.

AN EXPERIENCE OF MR. JOHN JONES.

IT happened sometime within the last ten or fifteen years, that, in my way through this troublesome world, I became captivated with the idea of starting a newspaper. That I had some talent for scribbling, I was vain enough to believe, and my estimate of the ability I possessed was sufficiently high to induce me to think that I could give a peculiar interest to the columns of a weekly paper, were such a publication entirely under my control.

I talked about the matter to a number of my literary and other friends, who, much to my satisfaction, saw all in a favourable light, and promised, if I would go on in the proposed enterprise, to use all their interest in my favour.

"I," said one, "will guaranty you fifty subscribers among my own circle of acquaintances."

"And I," said another, "am good for double that number."

"Put me down for a hundred more," said a third, and so the promises of support came like music to my willing ear.

One or two old veterans of the "press gang," to whom I spoke of my design, shrugged their shoulders, and said I had better try my hand at almost any thing else. But I was sanguine that I could succeed, though hundreds had failed before me. I felt that I possessed a peculiar fitness for the work, and could give a peculiar charm to a newspaper that would at once take it to the hearts and homes of the people.

A printer was called upon for an estimate, based upon a circulation of three thousand copies, which was set down as a very moderate expectation. He gave the whole cost of paper, composition, (type setting,) and press-work, at $4000.

This fell a little below my own roughly-made estimate, and settled my determinations. Two thousand copies, at two dollars a copy, which was to be the subscription price, would pay all the expenses, and if the number of subscribers rose to three thousand, of which there was not the shadow of a doubt in my mind, I would have a clear profit of $2000 the first year. And should it go to four thousand, as was most probable, my net income would be about $3400, for all increase would simply be chargeable with cost of paper and press-work—or about sixty cents on a subscriber. After the first year, of course there would be a steady increase in the number of subscribers, which, if at the rate of only a thousand a year, would give me in five years the handsome annual income of $9000. I was rich in prospective! Nothing could now hold me back. I ordered the printer to get ready his cases, and the paper-maker to provide, by a certain time, the paper.

As the terms were to be in advance, or rather the whole year payable at the expiration of the first quarter, I promised to begin paying cash for all contracts at the end of the first quarter. Up to this period of my life, I had gone on the strict principle of owing no man any thing, and I was known in the community where I lived to be a strictly honest and honourable man. Never having strained my credit, it was tight and strong, and I had but to ask the three months' favour to get it without a sign of reluctance.

Next I issued my prospectus for the "Literary Gazette and Weekly Reflex of Art, Literature, and Science, a Newspaper devoted to, &c. &c.," and scattered copies among my friends, expecting each to do his duty for me like a man. They were also posted in every book-store, hotel, and public place in the city. Said city, be it known, rejoiced in a population of a hundred thousand souls, of which number I saw no reason for doubting my ability to reach, with my interesting paper, at least three or four thousand, in the end. That was felt to be a very moderate calculation indeed. Then, when I turned my eyes over our vast country, with its millions and millions of intelligent, enlightened, reading and prosperous people, I felt that even to admit a doubt of success was a weakness for which I ought to be ashamed. And I wondered why, with such a harvest to reap, twenty such enterprises to one were not started.

While in this sanguine state, an individual who had been for thirty years a publisher and editor, prompted, as he said, by a sincere interest in my welfare, called to see me in order to give me the benefit of his experience. He asked me to state my views of the enterprise upon which I was about entering, which I did in glowing terms.

"Very well, Mr. Jones," said he, after I was done, "you base your calculations on three thousand subscribers?"

"I do," was my answer.

"From which number you expect to receive six thousand dollars."

"Certainly; the price of the paper is to be two dollars."

"I doubt, my young friend, very much, whether you will receive four thousand dollars from three thousand subscribers, if you should have that number. Nay, if you get three thousand during the year, you may be very thankful."

"Preposterous!" said I.

"No; not by any means. I have been over this ground before you, and know pretty much what kind of harvest it yields."

"But," said I, "it is not my intention to throw the paper into every man's house, whether he wants it or not. I will only take good subscribers."

"You would call Mr. B— —, over the way, a good subscriber, I presume?"

"Oh yes!" I replied, "I would very much like to have a few thousand like him."

"And Mr. Y— —, his next-door neighbour?"

"Yes—he is good, of course."

"That is, able to pay."

"And willing."

"I happen to know, my young friend, that neither of those men will pay a subscription to any thing if they can help it."

"Not to a work to which they have regularly subscribed?"

"No."

"That is as much as to say that they are dishonest men."

"You can say that or any thing else you please; I only give you the information for your own government. You will find a good many like them. Somehow or other, people seem to have a great aversion to paying newspaper bills. I don't know how it is, but such is the fact. And if you will take the advice of one who knows a good deal more about the business than you do, you will go to wood-sawing in preference to starting a newspaper. You *may* succeed, but in ten chances, there are nine on the side of failure."

I shrugged my shoulders and looked incredulous.

"Oh, very well!" said he, "go on and try for yourself. Bought wit is the best, if you don't pay too dear for it. You are young yet, and a little experience of this kind may do you no harm in the long run."

"I'm willing to take the risk, for I think I have counted the cost pretty accurately. As for a failure, I don't mean to know the word. There is a wide field of enterprise before me, and I intend to occupy it fully."

The old gentleman shrugged his shoulders in return, but volunteered no more of his good advice.

A week before the first number of the "Gazette and Reflex" was ready, I called in my prospectuses, in order to have the thousand or fifteen hundred names they contained regularly entered in the subscription-books with which I had provided myself. I had rented an office and employed a clerk. These were two items of expense that had not occurred to me when making my first calculation. It was rather a damper on the ardency of my hopes, to find, that instead of the large number of subscribers I had fondly expected to receive, the aggregate from all quarters was but two hundred!

One very active friend, who had guarantied me fifty himself, had but three names to his list; and another, who said I might set him down for a hundred, had not been able to do any thing, and, moreover, declined taking the paper himself, on the plea that he already took more magazines and newspapers than he could read or afford to pay for. Others gave as a reason for the little they had done, the want of a specimen number, and encouraged me with the assurance, that as soon as the paper appeared, there would be a perfect rush of subscribers.

In due time, the first number appeared, and a very attractive sheet it was—in my eyes. I took the first copy that came from the press, and, sitting down in my office, looked it over with a feeling of paternal pride, never before or since experienced. A more beautiful object, or rather one that it gave me more delight to view, had never been presented to my vision. If doubt had come in to disturb me, it all vanished now. To see the "Gazette and Reflex" would be enough. The two hundred "good names" on my list were felt to be ample for a start. Each copy circulated among those would bring from one to a dozen new subscribers. I regretted exceedingly that the type of the first form of the paper had been distributed. Had this not been the case, I would have ordered an additional thousand to be added to the three thousand with which I commenced my enterprise.

Saturday was the regular publication day of the paper, but I issued it on the preceding Wednesday. That is, served it to my two hundred subscribers and had it distributed to the daily press. With what eagerness did I look over the papers on Thursday morning, to see the glowing notices of my beautiful "Gazette and Reflex." I opened the first one that came to hand, glanced down column after column, but not a word about me or mine was there! A keener sense of disappointment I have never experienced. I took up another, and the first words that met my eyes were:

"We have received the first number of a new weekly paper started in this city, entitled the 'Literary Gazette and Weekly Reflex.' It is neat, and appears to be conducted with ability. It will, no doubt, receive a good share of patronage."

I threw aside the paper with an angry exclamation, and forthwith set the editor down as a jealous churl. In one or two other newspapers I found more extended and better notices; but they all fell so far short of the real merits of my bantling, that I was sadly vexed and disheartened. To have my advent announced so coldly and ungraciously, hurt me exceedingly. Still, I expected the mere announcement to bring a crowd of subscribers to my office; but, alas! only three presented themselves during the day. Generously enough, they paid down for the paper in advance, thus giving me six dollars, the first income from my new enterprise and the earnest of thousands that were soon to begin pouring in like a never-failing stream.

My friends called one after another, to congratulate me on the beautiful appearance of my paper, and to predict, for my encouragement, its widely extended popularity. I believed all they said, and more. But for all this, by the time the second number made its appearance, my list had only increased one hundred. Still, on reflection, this appeared very good, for at the rate of a hundred a week, I would have five thousand in a year.

"Why don't you employ canvassers?" inquired one. "There are hundreds in the city who will take the paper if it is only presented to them."

Acting on this hint, I advertised for men to solicit subscribers. Five of those who applied were chosen and distributed through five different sections of the city. I agreed to pay fifty cents for every good subscriber obtained. This was, of course, a pretty heavy drawback upon my expected income, but then it was admitted on all hands that a subscriber was worth fifty cents, as after he was once obtained he would doubtless remain a subscriber for years.

At the close of the first day my men brought in an average of ten subscribers each. The agreement was, that I was to pay them twenty-five cents on the name of a new subscriber being handed in, and the remaining twenty-five cents when the subscription due at the expiration of the first three months was collected. So I had twelve dollars and a half cash, to pay down. But then my list was increased to the extent of fifty names. The average of new subscribers from my agents continued for a couple of weeks, and then fell off sensibly. By the end of two months, my canvassers left the field, some of them sick of the business, and others tempted by more promising inducements.

Many of the country papers noticed my "Gazette and Reflex" in the most flattering manner, and not a few of them copied my prospectus. This had the effect to bring me in a few hundred subscribers by mail, with the cash, in a large number of cases in advance. About one-third, however, promised to remit early.

At the end of three months, according to promise, I was to pay my printer and paper maker. Up to that time my cash receipts had been three hundred dollars, but every cent was gone. My clerk had to be paid seven dollars a week regularly, and a mail and errand boy, three dollars. Advertising had cost me twenty-five dollars; account and subscription books as much more; and I had paid over fifty dollars to my agents for getting subscribers. Besides, there had been a dozen little et ceteras of expense, not before taken into calculation. Moreover, out of this three hundred dollars of income I had my own personal expenses to pay.

In the thirteenth number of my paper, I gave notice that the three months having expired, all subscriptions were due for the year according to the terms, and called upon subscribers "to step to the captain's office and settle." There were of unpaid subscribers now upon my books the number of five hundred and forty, and my debt to printer and paper maker was exactly nine hundred and eighty dollars, I having kept on printing three thousand copies, under the belief that the list must go up to that.

Day after day went by after this notice appeared, yet not a single man answered to the invitation. I began to feel serious. Subscribers continued to come in, though slowly, and people all spoke highly of the paper and said it must succeed. But its success, so far, was not over flattering. Finding that people would not take the plain hint I had given, I went over the books and made out all the bills. One thousand and eighty dollars was the aggregate amount due. These bills, except those for the country, I placed in the hands of a collector, and told him to get me in the money as quickly as possible. Those for the country, about one hundred in number, I enclosed in the paper. On the faith of this proceeding, I promised the paper maker and printer each two hundred dollars in a couple of weeks.

Four days elapsed without my collector making his appearance, greatly to my surprise. On the fifth day I met him in the street.

"Well, how are you coming on?" said I.

"Oh, slowly," he replied.

"I expected to see you a day or two ago."

"I had nothing of consequence to return. But I will be in on Saturday."

I felt a kind of choking in my throat as I turned away. On Saturday the collector called—he opened his memorandum-book, and I my cash-book, preparatory to making entries of money returned.

"Mr. A— —," said the collector, "says he never pays in advance for any thing."

"But the terms of the paper are in advance after the first three months."

"I know."

"Did you call his attention to this?"

"Oh, yes! but he said he didn't care for your terms. He'd been swindled once or twice by paying in advance, but never intended to give anybody the opportunity to do the same thing again."

Mr. A— —was a man whom I had known for years. I cannot tell how hurt and indignant I was at such language. He took my paper, knowing the terms upon which it was published, and when I sent my bill, refused to comply with the terms, and insulted me into the bargain. I turned to his name on the subscription-book, and striking it off, said—

"He can't have the paper."

"Credit Mr. B— —with six months and discontinue," said the collector, as he passed to the next name on his list. Mr. B— —was a man whom I knew very well by reputation. I had looked upon him as one of my best subscribers. He was a merchant in easy circumstances.

"Why does he wish it stopped?" I asked.

"He says he merely took the paper by way of encouraging the enterprise, and never supposed he would be called upon to pay for it. He told Mr. J— —, who asked him to subscribe, that he had more papers now than he wanted, and Mr. J— —said, No matter. He would have it sent to him by way of adding another respectable name to the list."

"Very well," said I, as I entered the name of Mr. B— —in the cash-book, "pass on."

This went fairly ahead of any thing I had ever dreamed of. I was too much surprised even to make a remark on the subject.

"Mr. C—-was as mad as a March hare when I presented his bill."

"Indeed! Why?"

"He paid your agent when he subscribed!"

"Did you see his receipt?"

"Yes. The agent took a hat and paid him the difference."

"The scoundrel! And charged me a quarter in addition, for returning the subscriber!"

"These canvassers are a slippery set."

"That's swindling!"

"The fellow won't quarrel with you about the terms, seeing that he enjoys the hat."

"Too bad! Too bad! Well, go on."

Mr. D——paid two dollars, but wants you to stop at the end of the year. He merely took a copy at the start by way of encouraging the enterprise. Thinks highly of the paper, but can't afford to take it longer than a year."

"Very well."

"Mr. E—-has paid."

"Well?"

"Mr. F——says he never subscribed, and does not want it. He says, if you will send to his house, you can get all the numbers. He told the carrier not to leave it from the first."

"I paid an agent for his name."

"He says he told the agent that he didn't want the paper. That he took more now than he could read."

"Swindled again!"
"Mr. G——says he never saw the paper in his life."

"It's sent regularly."

"Some mistake in the carrier. Mr. H——paid, and wishes the paper discontinued."

"Very well."

"Mr. I——says he can't afford to take it. His name was put down without his consent."

I had received this name through one of my kind friends.

"Mr. J——paid a dollar, and wants it stopped."

"Well?"

"Mr. K——paid; also, Mr. L——and Mr. M——."

"Well?"

"Mr. N——says the paper is not left for him; but for a young man who has gone West. Thinks you had better stop it."

I erased the name.

Mr. O——-paid the agent."

"He never returned the money."

Mr. P——and Mr. Q——, ditto."

"Never saw a copper of their money. Paid a quarter apiece, cash, for each of these subscribers."

"Mr. R——says the paper is not worth reading. That he wouldn't pay a shilling a year for it. I advise you to stop it. He never pays for any thing if he can help it. Mr. S——paid. Mr. T——paid up to this date, and wishes it stopped. Never ordered it. Mr. U——paid. I called upon a great many more, but they put me off with one excuse or other. I never had a much worse lot of bills."

A basin of cold water on a sentimental serenader could not have produced a greater revulsion of feeling than did this unlooked-for return of my collector. Nineteen dollars and fifty cents, instead of about two hundred dollars, were all he had been able to gather up; there was no promise of success in the future on any different scale. I received the money, less ten per cent. for collecting, and was left alone to my own reflections. Not of the most pleasant kind, the reader may well imagine. For an hour I brooded over the strangely embarrassing position in which I found myself, and then, after thinking until my head was hot and my feet and hands cold, I determined to reduce, immediately, the edition of my paper from three thousand to one thousand, and thus save an item of thirty dollars a week in paper and press-work. To send off my clerk, also, to whom I was paying seven dollars weekly, and with the aid of a boy, attend to the office, and do the writing and mailing myself. I then went over the subscription-book, and counted up the names. The number was just seven hundred and twenty. I had but a little while before replied to a question on the subject, that I had about twelve hundred on my list. And I did vaguely imagine that I had that number. I knew better now.

To describe minutely the trials, sufferings, and disappointments of the whole year, would take too much time and space. The subsequent returns of my collector were about on a par with the first. Finding it impossible to pay the printer and paper maker, as promised, out of the advance subscriptions falling due at the end of three months, I borrowed from some of my friends about four hundred dollars, and paid it over, stating, when I did so, that I must have a new contract, based upon a six months' credit.

I found no great difficulty in obtaining this from the paper maker, to whom I spoke in confident terms of my certain ultimate success. The printer required half cash, which I agreed to pay.

This arrangement I fondly hoped would give me time to make my collections, and, besides paying off the debt already accumulated, enable me to acquire a surplus to meet the notes given, from time to time, for paper and printing.

At the end of a year, my list, through various exertions and sacrifices, had arisen to twelve hundred. On this I had collected eight hundred dollars, and I calculated that there were about sixteen hundred dollars due me, which, I thought, if all collected in, would about square me up with the world. This I thought. But, when I came to go over my bill-book and ledger, I found, to my utter dismay, that I owed three thousand five hundred dollars! This must be a mistake, I said, and went over my books again. The result was as at first. I owed the money, and no mistake. But how it was, I could not for some time comprehend. But a series of memorandums from my cash-book, and an examination of printers' and paper makers' bills, at length made all clear. I had used, on my own personal account, four hundred dollars during the year. Office rent was two hundred and fifty. My carriers had cost over a hundred dollars. My boy one hundred and fifty, and ninety had been paid to the clerk during the first three months. Sundry little items of expense during the year made an aggregate of over a hundred. Paper and printing for the first three months had been nearly a thousand dollars, and for the last three quarters about twenty-two hundred dollars.

To go on with this odds against me, I had sense enough to see was perfect folly. But, how could I stop? I was not worth a dollar in the world; and the thought of wronging those who had trusted me in full reliance upon my integrity, produced a feeling of suffocation. Besides, I had worked for a year as few men work. From sunrise until twelve, one, and two o'clock, I was engaged in the business or editorial duties appertaining to my enterprise, and to abandon all after such a struggle was disheartening.

After much deliberation, I concluded that the best thing I could do was to sell out my list of subscribers to another and more successful establishment in the city, and, for this purpose, waited upon the publisher. He heard me, and after I had finished, asked my terms. I told him fifteen hundred dollars for the list. He smiled, and said he wouldn't give me five hundred for the whole concern, debts and all. I got up, put on my hat, and left him with indignant silence.

To go on was the worst horn for me to grasp in the dilemma in which I found myself. To stop, would be to do so with some three or four hundred persons paid in advance, for portions of a year. I was dunned, daily, by my printer, for money, and in order to meet the notes which had already fallen due, I had been compelled to borrow temporarily from my friends. Unable to arrive at any satisfactory conclusion, in despair, I summoned creditors and friends around me, and laid before them a full statement of my condition. There were some long faces at that meeting; but no one felt as I did. I shall never forget the suffering and mortification of that day, were I to live a thousand years.

The unanimous determination of the meeting was that I must stop, collect in the money due, and divide it pro rata among my creditors. I did so; announcing, at the same time, the heavy embarrassment under which I had been brought, and earnestly soliciting those who owed the paper, to settle their accounts immediately. To the few who had paid the fraction of a year in advance, I stated how much I had lost, and appealed to their magnanimity for a remission of the obligation I remained under to furnish the paper for the time yet due to them. It was but the matter of a few cents, or a dollar at most to them, I said, but it was hundreds of dollars to me.

Well, and what was the sequel to all this? Why, to sum up what remains to be told, in a few words; only two hundred dollars out of the sixteen hundred were collected, and from those who had paid small trifles in advance, I received dozens of letters, couched in the most offensive terms. Some charged me with being a swindler, and said, if I didn't immediately send the money overpaid, or some other paper in the place of mine, they would publish me to the world. Others said they would be in the city at a certain time and require me to refund; while many, residing on the spot, took out their money's worth, by telling me to my face what they thought of my conduct. One man issued a warrant against me for thirty-five cents, the sum overpaid by him.

So much for my experience in starting a newspaper. A year and a half before, I had a clerkship which brought me in seven hundred dollars a year; was easy in mind, respected by all my friends, looked upon as an honest man by every one who knew me, and out of debt. I started a newspaper in a moment of blind infatuation, and now I owed above three thousand dollars, my good name was gone, and I was dispirited, out of employment, afraid to walk the street lest I should encounter some one I owed, and as wretched as a man could well be. I soon after left the city, and sought employment hundreds of miles away. So much for my experience in starting a newspaper.

THE WAY OF TRANSGRESSORS.

"Do not go out to-night, Amanda. The pavements are damp, and the air is loaded with vapour."

"Indeed, ma, I must go."

"Amanda, there is no necessity for your attending this party; and very urgent reasons why you should stay at home. Your cough is still troublesome, and a little exposure might give it permanency. You know that from your father you inherit a predisposition to disease of the lungs."

"You only say that to alarm me."

"Not so, my child; I know your constitution, and know how fatally the exposure of a night like this may affect you."

"But I'll wrap up warmly, and put on my India rubbers."

"A necessary precaution, if you will go out, Amanda. But I wish I could persuade you to be guided by me. You know that the Bible says, the way of transgressors is hard."

"I don't know how you will apply that to me, ma. I am transgressing no law of divine appointment."

"Be not sure of that, Amanda."

"I do not understand you, ma."

"I will try and make my meaning clear. In our creation, as organized beings, we were so constituted as to bear a certain relation to every thing around us, and our bodily health was made dependent upon this relation. Here then, we have a law of health, which may be called a divine law—for there is nothing good that does not flow from the Divine Creator. If we violate this law, we become transgressors, and shall certainly prove the way we have chosen, in so doing, to be a hard one."

"Oh, is that all?" said the daughter, looking up with a smile, and breathing more freely. "I'll risk the consequences of breaking the law you have announced."

"Amanda!"

"Don't be so serious, ma. I will wrap up close and have my feet well protected. There is not the least danger of my taking cold."

"Well, you must do as you please. Still I cannot approve of your going, for I see that there is danger. But you are fully of age, and I will not seek to control you."

So strong was Amanda's desire to attend a large but select party, that she went, in company with a young man who called for her, notwithstanding the atmosphere was so humid and dense with fog, that breathing became oppressive.

The rooms were crowded, and the air in them so warm as to cause the perspiration to start from the fair brows of the merry dancers, among whom none was more fair or more lively than Amanda Beaufort. At eleven, after having passed an evening of much pleasure, she started for home with her companion. She was so well wrapped up, that she did not feel the cold, and her feet were protected from the damp pavement by the impervious India rubber.

"I'm safe home, ma, after all!" she exclaimed with her merry ringing laugh, as she bounded into the chamber where her ever-watchful and interested mother sat awaiting her daughter's return.

"I am glad to see you back, Amanda," said Mrs. Beaufort kindly, "and hope that no ill consequences will follow what I must still call a very imprudent act."

"Oh I'm just as well as ever, and have not taken the least cold. How could I, wrapped up so warm?"

Still, on the next morning, unaccountable as it was to Amanda, she was quite hoarse, and was much troubled by a cough occasioned by a slight but constant tickling in her throat. Accompanying these symptoms was a pale anxious face and a general feeling of lassitude.

"I feared all this, Amanda," said her mother, with manifest concern.

"It's only a slight cold, ma. And, anyhow, I don't believe it was occasioned by going out last night, I was wrapped up so warm. I must have got the bed-clothes off of me in the night."

"What to one is a slight cold, my daughter, is a very serious affair to another; and you are one of those who can never take a slight cold without shocking the whole system. Your pale face and your evident debility this morning show how much even this slight cold, as you call it, has affected you. That you have this cold is to me no subject of wonder. You were well wrapped up, it is true, and your feet protected. Still, your face was exposed, and every particle of air you inhaled was teeming with moisture. From dancing in a warm room, the pores of your skin were all opened, and the striking of moist chilly air upon your face could hardly fail of producing some degree of cold. The most susceptible parts of your body are your throat and lungs, and to these any shock which is received by the system is directly conveyed. You cannot take cold in your hand or foot or face, or any other part of your body, without your breast sympathizing;— that you are hoarse, and have a slight cough, then, is to me in no way surprising."

Amanda tried to make light of this, but every hour she felt worse and worse. Her hoarseness, instead of diminishing, increased, and her cough grew more and more troublesome. Finally, she was compelled to go to bed, and have the physician called in.—"Is there any danger?" asked Mrs. Beaufort, with an anxious and troubled countenance, as the physician, after prescribing among other things a stimulating application to the throat externally, was about leaving the house.

"Is your daughter subject to these fits of hoarseness, ma'am?" he asked.

"Yes, sir, whenever she takes cold."

"And does that frequent irritating cough always attend the recurrence of hoarseness?"

"Always."

"Then, madam, it is but right that you should know, that such results, following a slight cold, indicate a very great tendency to pulmonary or bronchial affections. The predisposition existing, very great care should be taken to prevent all exciting causes. With care, your daughter may retain her health until she passes over the most critical portion in the life of every one with such a constitution as hers—that is, from twenty years of age until thirty or thirty-five.

Without great care and prudence during that time, her constitution may be shattered so as to set all remedial efforts at defiance."

"But, doctor, how is she now?" was Mrs. Beaufort's anxious inquiry.

"Not dangerous, madam, but still in a condition requiring care and skill to prevent unfavourable consequences."

"Then do your best for her, doctor."

"You can rely on me for that, Mrs. Beaufort. Good morning."

With a heavy heart the mother returned to the sick chamber of her daughter, and sat down by the bedside, thoughtfully, for a few moments, while she held Amanda's hand, that was hot with fever. Then recollecting herself, she left the room to prepare the stimulating application which had been ordered.

It is remarkable how the whole system will sympathize with one diseased part. The cold which Amanda had taken concentrated its active effects upon her respiratory organs; but it was felt also in every member, prostrating the whole body, and giving a sensation of general suffering. Her head ached violently, and a burning fever diffused itself over the entire surface of her body.

How sadly was she proving the truth of her mother's warning, when she said to her, in the language of divine authority, "The way of transgressors is hard."

She had violated a law of health, and in that violation, as in the violation of every physical or moral law, the penalty of transgression followed too surely.

It was a week before Amanda was able to go about again, and then her pale cheeks, and debilitated frame indicated but too plainly the sad consequences of a single imprudent act.

A few weeks after she had become restored apparently to her usual health, as Amanda was dressing one morning to go out, her mother said—

"Your clothes are a great deal too tight, Amanda."

"Oh no, I am not tight at all, ma. Julia Mason laces as tight again. She gets her sister to draw her lacings for her, and she has to pull with all her strength."

"That is wrong in Julia Mason, and yet half the pressure that she can bear would seriously injure you."

"How can that be, ma? I am as healthy as she is."

"I will tell you, Amanda. She has a full round chest, giving free play to the lungs; while your chest is narrow and flat. Without any compression, the action of your lungs is not so free and healthy as hers would be, laced as tightly as you say she laces. But when to your natural conformation you add artificial pressure, the action of your lungs becomes not only enfeebled, but the unhealthy action induced tends to develop that peculiar form of disease, the predisposition to which you inherit."

"That is only an idea of yours, ma. I am sure I have quite a full bust," said Amanda, glancing down at her chest, and embracing it with her hands.

"There you are mistaken. I have noticed this defect, with much anxiety, ever since you were a child; and having had my attention called to it, have frequently made comparisons, and have found that you are remarkably narrow and flat, and what is more, have a tendency to stoop, which still lessens the size of the cavity in which the lungs play."

"Well, ma, my clothes are not tight. Just see here."

Mrs. Beaufort tried her clothes, and found them to be much tighter than in her judgment was good for health.

"You are still unwilling, Amanda, to be governed by your mother, where her wishes come in opposition to your pride or inclinations. I know that you are compressing your chest too much, but you are not willing to yield to my judgment. And yet I prescribe no arbitrary rules, but endeavor to guide you by a rational consideration of true principles. These you will not see; and the consequences that must follow their violation will be the transgressor's reward."

"Indeed, indeed, ma, you are too serious. You are frightened at a shadow. No one of my friends enjoys better general health than I do."

"And so might the graceful maple say of the sturdy oak in the first years of their existence. But long after the first had been humbled beneath the hand of decay, the other would stand with its roots more firmly imbedded in the earth, and its limbs battling the storms as vigorously as ever."

Amanda made no reply to this, for she was suddenly struck with its force. Still she only pretended to loosen her stays to satisfy her mother, while the lacings remained as tense as ever.

It is unnecessary to trace, step by step, the folly of Amanda Beaufort through a series of years—years that caused her mother much and painful anxiety—up to her twenty-sixth summer, when, as a wife and mother, she was suffering the penalty of her indiscretion, proving too clearly the truth, that the way of transgressors is hard. In spite of all her mother's warnings and remonstrances, she had continued to expose herself to the night air in damp weather—to attend balls thinly clad, and remain at them to a very late hour, and to lace herself so tightly as to seriously retard the healthy action of the vital organs. At the age of twenty-three she married. A year after, the birth of a child gave her whole system, which had indicated long before its feebleness, a powerful shock, from which the reaction was slow and unsteady. The colour never came back to her cheek, nor the elasticity to her frame. She had so long subjected herself to the pressure of an artificial external support, that she could not leave off her stays without experiencing such a sinking, sickening sensation, as she called it, that she was compelled to continue, however reluctantly, the compression and support of tightly-laced corsets. And from frequently taking cold, through imprudence, the susceptibility had become so great, that the slightest dampness of the feet or the exposure to a light draught of air was sure to bring on a cough of hoarseness. Her nervous system, too, was sadly shattered. Indeed, every indication presented, foreshadowed a rapid and premature decline—consequent, solely, upon her thoughtless imprudence in earlier years.

"Shall I never feel any better, ma?" asked Amanda, one day, as a faint sickness came over her, compelling her to resign her dear little babe into the arms of its nurse, looking up at the same time so earnestly and appealingly into her mother's face, that Mrs. Beaufort's heart was touched with unwonted sorrow and tenderness.

"I hope so, Amanda," was replied, but in a tone that, though meant to encourage, conveyed little hope to the bosom of her child.

"Every time little Anna nurses, I feel so sick and faint, that, sometimes, it seems that I must give up. And yet the thought of letting the dear little angel draw her food from another bosom than mine, makes me fainter and sicker still. Can nothing be done to help me, ma?"

"We must see the doctor and consult with him. Perhaps he can do something," Mrs. Beaufort replied, in an abstracted tone.

That day the family physician was called in, and a long consultation held. The result was, a decision that Amanda must get a nurse for her child, and then try the effect upon her system of a change of air and the use of medicinal waters. In a word, she must put away her child and go to the Springs.

"Indeed, doctor, I cannot give up little Anna," said the invalid mother, while the tears started to her eyes. "I will be very careful of myself, and teach her to take a little food early, so as to relieve me as much as possible. It seems as if it would kill me, were I forced to resign to a stranger a mother's dearest privilege and holiest duty."

"I can but honour your devotion to your child, Amanda," the old family physician said, with a tenderness unusual to one whose daily intercourse was with suffering in its varied forms. "Still, I am satisfied, that for every month you nurse that babe, a year is taken from your life."

There was in the tone and manner of the doctor a solemn emphasis, that instantly aroused the young husband's liveliest fears, and sent a chill to the heart of Mrs. Beaufort.

For a moment or two, Amanda's thoughts were turned inward, and then looking up with a smile of strange meaning, while her eyes grew brighter, and something like a glow kindled upon her thin, pale cheek, she said, drawing her babe at the same time closer to her bosom —

"I will risk all, doctor. I cannot forego a mother's duty."

"A mother's duty, my dear young friend," the physician replied, with increased tenderness, for his heart was touched, "is to prolong, by every possible means, her own life, for the sake of her offspring. There are duties which none but a mother can perform. Reserve yourself for these, Amanda, and let others do for your babe all that can be done as well as you can perform it. Take my advice. Leave little Anna at home with your mother and a careful nurse; and then, with your husband and some female friend, upon whose judicious care you can rely, go to the Springs and spend a few weeks."

The advice of the physician was taken, and the young mother, with clinging, though lacerated affections, resigned to the care of a hired nurse the babe over which her heart yearned with unutterable tenderness.

Three weeks were spent at one of the Virginia springs, but little apparent benefit was the result. The young mother grieved for the loss of her babe so deeply and constantly, often giving way to tears, that the renovating effects of changed air and medicinal waters were counteracted, and she returned home, drooping in body and depressed in spirits. Her infant seemed but half restored to her, as she clasped it to a bosom in which the current of its young life had been dried up. Sad, sad indeed was her realization of the immutable truth, that the way of transgressors is hard!

Two years more of a painful and anxious existence were eked out, and Amanda again became a mother.

From this additional shock she partially recovered; but it soon became evident to all, that her shattered and enfeebled constitution was rapidly giving way. Her last babe was but four months old, when the pale messenger passed by, and gave his fearful summons.

It was toward the close of one of those calm days in September, when nature seems pausing to note the first few traces of decay which autumn has thrown upon garden, field, and forest, that Mrs. Beaufort, and the husband of her daughter, with a few friends, were gathered in the chamber of their beloved one, to see her die. How sad, how very sad is the death-bed of the young, sinking beneath premature decay! In the passing away of one who has met the storms of life, and battled with them through vigorous maturity, and sinks at last in the course of nature, there is little to pain the feelings. But when the young and beautiful die, with all their tenderest and earliest ties clinging to them—an event so unlooked for, so out of the true order of nature—we can only turn away and weep. We can extract from such an affliction but few thoughts of comfort. All is dreary, and blank, and desolate.

"Bring me my children," the dying mother said, rousing up from a state of partial slumber, with an earnest emphasis, that brought both her mother and her husband to her bedside.

"What did you want, dear Amanda?" asked the husband, laying his hand gently upon her white forehead, that was damp with the dews of coming dissolution.

"My dear babes," she replied in a changed tone, rising up with an effort. "My Anna and Mary. Who will be a mother to them, when I am laid at rest? Oh, that I could take them with me!"

Tears came to the relief of her overwrought feelings, and leaning her head upon the breast of her husband, she wept and sobbed aloud. The infant was brought in by her mother, and laid in her arms, when she had a little recovered herself.

"Oh, my baby! my sweet baby!" she said, with tender animation. "My sweet, sweet baby! I cannot give you up!" And she clasped it to her breast with an energy of affection, while the large drops rolled over her pale cheek. "And Anna, dear little girl! where is my Anna?" she asked.

Anna, a beautiful child, a few months past her second birth-day, was brought in and lifted upon the bed.

"Don't cry, ma," said the little thing, seeing the tears upon her mother's cheeks, "don't cry; I'll always be good."

"Heaven bless you and keep you, my child!" the mother sobbed, eagerly kissing the sweet lips that were turned up to hers; and then clasped the child to her bosom in a strong embrace.

The children were, after a time, removed, but the thoughts of the dying mother were still upon them; and with these thoughts were self-reproach, that made her pillow one of thorns.

"I now see and feel," said she, looking up into the face of her mother, after having lain with closed eyes for about ten minutes, "that all my sufferings, and this early death, which will soon be upon me, would have been avoided, if I had only permitted myself to be guided by you. I do not wonder now that my constitution gave way. How could it have been otherwise, and I so strangely regardless of all the laws of health? But, my dear mother, the past is beyond recall; and now I leave to you the dear little ones from whom I must soon part for ever. I feel calmer than I have felt for some time. The bitterness of the last agony seems over. But I do not see you, nor you, dear husband! Give me your hands. Here, let my head rest on your bosom. It is sweet to lie thus—Anna—dear child! Mary—sweet, sweet babe!"—

The lips of the young wife and mother moved feebly, and inarticulate whispers fell faintly from her tongue for some moments, and then she sank to sleep—and it was a sleep from which none wake in the body.

Thus, at the age of twenty-six, abused and exhausted nature gave up the struggle; and the mother, who had violated the laws of health, sank to the earth just at the moment when her tenderest and holiest duties called loudest for performance.

Who, in this brief and imperfect sketch, does not recognise familiar features? Amanda Beaufort is but one of a class which has far too many representatives. These are in every town and village, in every street and neighbourhood. Why do we see so many pale-faced mothers? Why are our young and lovely females so soon broken down under their maternal duties? The answer, in far too many cases, may be found in their early and persevering transgression of the most palpable physiological laws. The violation of these is ever followed, sooner or later, in a greater or less degree, by painful consequences. Sometimes life is spared to the young mother, and she is allowed to linger on through years of suffering that the heart aches to think of. Often death terminates early her pains, and her babes are left a legacy to the cold charities of an unfeeling world. How sad, how painful the picture! Alas! that it is a true one.

JUST GOING TO DO IT.

EVERY man has some little defect of character, some easily-besetting sin that is always overtaking him, unless he be ever on the alert. My friend, Paul Burgess, was a man of considerable force of mind; whatever he undertook was carried through with much energy of purpose. But his leading defect was a tendency to inertia in small matters. It required an adequate motive to put the machinery of his mind in operation. Some men never let a day pass without carefully seeing after every thing, little or great, that ought to be done. They cannot rest until the day's work is fully completed. But it was very different with Paul. If the principal business transactions of the day were rightly performed, he was satisfied to let things of less consideration lie over until another time. From this cause it occurred that every few weeks there was an accumulation of things necessary to be done, so great that their aggregate calls upon his attention roused him to action, and then every thing was reduced to order with an energy, promptness, and internal satisfaction that made him wonder at himself for ever having neglected these minor interests so long. On these occasions, a firm resolution was always made never again to let a day come to its close without every thing being done that the day called for. It usually happened that the first hour did not pass after the forming of this resolution without seeing its violation—so strong was the power of habit growing out of an original defect in the mind.

Every consequence in life is the natural result of some cause, and upon the character of the cause always depends the nature of the consequence. An orderly cause never produces a disorderly consequence, and the converse of this is equally true. Every defect of character that we have, no matter how small and seemingly insignificant it may be, if suffered to flow down into our actions, produces an evil result. The man who puts off the doing of a thing until to-morrow that ought to be done to-day, injures his own interest or the interest of others. This may not always clearly show itself, but the fact is nevertheless true. Sometimes the consequences of even the smallest neglect are felt most deeply.

My friend Paul had a very familiar saying when reminded by any one of something that ought to have been previously done. "I was just going to do it," or "I am just going to do it," dropped from his tongue half-a-dozen times in a day.

"I wish you would have my bill ready by three o'clock," said a customer to him, dropping in one morning.

"Very well, it shall be made out," replied Paul.

The customer turned and walked hurriedly away. He evidently had a good deal of business to do, and but a small time to do it in.

Precisely at three, the man called, and found the merchant reading the afternoon paper.

"Is my bill made out?" he asked.

"I am just going to do it," answered Paul, handing the paper towards his customer. "Look over the news for a few moments while I draw it off; it won't take me long."

"I am sorry," replied the customer, "for I cannot wait. I have three or four more accounts to settle, and the boat leaves in an hour. Send me the bill by mail, and I will remit you the amount. Good-by" — offering his hand — "I hope to see you again in the fall."

Paul took the extended hand of his customer, and shook it warmly. In the next moment he was standing alone, his ledger open before him, and his eye resting upon an account, the payment of which was of some importance to him just at that time. Disappointed and dissatisfied with himself, he closed the ledger heavily and left the desk, instead of making out the account and mailing it. On the next day, the want of just the amount of money he would have received from his customer kept him on the street two hours. It was three weeks before he made out the account and sent it on. A month elapsed, but no remittance came. He dropped his customer a line, and received for answer that when last in the city he had bought more goods than he intended, and consequently paid away all his cash; business had not yet begun to stir, and thus far what little he had sold had been for credit, but that he hoped soon to make him a remittance. The next news Paul had of his customer was that he had failed.

It was said of him that when a young man he became quite enamoured of a reigning belle, who to great beauty added many far more essential prerequisites in a good wife, not the least of which in the eye of Paul was a handsome fortune left her by a distant relative.

To this young lady he paid very marked attentions for some time, but he did not stand alone in the number of her admirers. Several others were as much interested in gaining her favourable regard as he was.

One day a friend said to him—"Paul, have you heard the news?"

"What is it?"

Sefton has offered himself to Miss P— —."

"It a'n't possible! Why, I was just going to do it myself! Has she accepted him?"

"So it is said."

"I don't believe it."

"I don't know how you will ascertain, certainly, unless you ask the lady herself," replied the friend.

"I will find out within an hour, if I have to do what you suggest. Sefton offered himself! I declare, I didn't dream that any particular intimacy existed between them. My own mind has been made up these two or three months—in fact, long before Sefton knew her; but I have kept procrastinating the offer of marriage I determined to make, week after week, like a fool as I am, until I have allowed another to step in and carry off the prize, if what you say be true. But I can't believe it. I am sure Miss P— —wouldn't accept any man on so short an acquaintance."

"Sefton is a bold fellow, and prompt in all his movements," returned the friend. "I rather think you will find the report true. I know that he has been paying her the closest attentions."

"I won't believe a word of it until I have undoubted evidence of the fact. It can't be!" said Paul, pacing the floor in considerable perturbation of mind.

But it was all so, as he very soon ascertained, to his deep regret and mortification at allowing another to carry off the prize he had thought his own. When next under the influence of the tender passion, my friend took good care to do in good time just what he was going to do.

Paul was perfectly aware of his defect, and often made the very best resolutions against it, but it generally happened that they were broken as soon as made. It was so easy to put off until the next hour, or until to-morrow, a little thing that might just as well be done now. Generally, the thing to be done was so trifling in itself, that the effort to do it appeared altogether disproportionate at the time. It was like exerting the strength of a giant to lift a pebble.

Sometimes the letters and papers would accumulate upon his desk for a week or ten days, simply because the effort to put away each letter as it was read and answered, and each paper as it was used, seemed so great when compared with the trifling matter to be accomplished, as to appear a waste of effort, notwithstanding time enough would be spent in reading the newspapers, conversation, or sitting idly about, to do all this three or four times over. When confusion reached its climax, then he would go to work most vigorously, and in a few hours reduce all to order. But usually some important paper was lost or mislaid, and could not be found at the time when most needed. It generally happened that this great effort was not made until he had been going to do it for three or four days, and not then until the call for some account or other commercial paper, which was nowhere to be found, made a thorough examination of what had been accumulating for some time in his drawers and on his desk necessary. He was not always fortunate in discovering the object of his search.

Notwithstanding this minor defect in Paul's character, his great shrewdness and thorough knowledge of business made him a successful merchant. In matters of primary interest, he was far-seeing, active, and prompt, and as these involved the main chance, his worldly affairs were prosperous. Whatever losses he encountered were generally to be traced to his neglect of little matters in the present, to his habit of "going to do," but never doing at the right time.

Not only in his business, but in his domestic affairs, and in every thing that required his attention, did this disposition to put off the doing of little things show itself. The consequences of his neglect were always disturbing him in one way or another. So long as he alone suffered, no one had a right to complain; but it is not to be supposed that such a fault as he was chargeable with could exist and not affect others.

One day while Paul was at his desk, a young lady, dressed in deep mourning, came into his store and asked to see him. The clerk handed her back to where his principal was sitting, who bowed low to the stranger and offered her a chair. The young lady drew aside her veil as she seated herself, and showed a young and beautiful face that was overcast with a shade of sadness. Although Paul never remembered having seen the young lady before, he could not help remarking that there was something very familiar in her countenance.

"My name is Miss Ellison," said the stranger, in a low, tremulous voice. "I believe you know my mother, sir."

"Oh, very well," quickly returned Paul. "You are not Lucy Ellison, surely?"

"Yes, sir, my name is Lucy," returned the young lady.

"Can it be possible? Why, it seems but yesterday that you were a little girl. How rapidly time flies! How is your mother, Miss Ellison? She is one of my old friends."

"She is well, I thank you, sir," Lucy replied, casting her eyes timidly to the floor.

There was a pause. While Paul was turning over in his mind what next to say, and slightly wondering what could be the cause of this visit, the young lady said, "Mr. Burgess, my mother desired me to call upon you to ask your interest in procuring me the situation of French teacher in Mr. C——'s school. Since my father's death, our means of living have become so much reduced that it is necessary for me to do something to prevent absolute want from overtaking us."

Lucy's voice trembled very much, and once or twice a choking sensation in her throat prevented the utterance of a word; but she strove resolutely with herself, and was able to finish what she wished to say more calmly.

"I am perfectly ready," she continued, "to do any thing that lies in my power. The French language I have studied thoroughly, and having enjoyed the friendship and been on terms of intimacy with two or three French ladies of education, I believe I can speak the language with great accuracy. Mother says she knows you to be on intimate terms with Mr. C— —, and that a word from you will secure me the situation."

"Mr. C— —is, then, in want of a French teacher?"

"Oh, yes," replied Lucy; "we learned the fact yesterday. The salary is five hundred dollars, which will give us a comfortable support if I can obtain the situation."

"Of which there can be no doubt, Miss Ellison," returned Paul, "if your qualifications are such as to meet the approval of Mr. C— —, which I presume they are. I will certainly call upon him and secure you the place, if possible. Tell your mother that if in this or in any other way I can serve either you or her, I will do it with sincere pleasure. Please take to her my kind regards."

Lucy warmly expressed her thanks. On rising to depart, she said, "When shall I call in, Mr. Burgess, to hear the result of your interview with Mr. C— —?"

"You needn't give yourself the trouble of calling at all, Miss Ellison," replied Mr. Burgess. "The moment I have seen the person of whom we were speaking, I will either call upon your mother or send her a note."

"You are very kind," dropped almost involuntarily from Lucy's lips, as, with a graceful inclination of her body, she drew her veil over her face, and, turning from the merchant, walked quickly away.

When Paul went home at dinner-time, he said to his wife, "I am sure you couldn't guess who I had for a visitor this morning."

"Then of course it would be useless for me to try," replied the wife, smiling. "Who was it?"

"You know the Ellisons?"

"Yes."

"Mr. Ellison, you remember, died about a year ago."

"Yes."

"At the time of his death it was rumoured that his estate was involved, but never having had any business transactions with him, I had no occasion to investigate the matter, and did not really know what had been the result of its settlement. This morning I was greatly surprised to receive a visit from Lucy Ellison, who had grown up into a beautiful young woman."

"Indeed!" ejaculated the wife. "And what did she want?"

"She came at her mother's request to solicit my influence with Mr. C——, who is in want of a French teacher. She said that their circumstances were very much changed since her father's death and that it had become necessary for her to do something as a means of supporting the family. The salary given by Mr. C——to his French teacher is five hundred dollars. I really pitied the young thing from my heart. Think of our Mary, in two or three years from this, when, if ever, a cloudless sky should bend over her, going to some old friend of her father's, and almost tearfully soliciting him to beg for her, of another, the privilege of toiling for bread. It made my heart ache."

"She must be very young," remarked Mrs. Burgess.

"Not over eighteen or nineteen."

"Poor thing! What a sad, sad change she must feel it to be! But did you call upon Mr. C——?"

A slight shade passed over the countenance of Paul.

"Not yet," he replied.

"Oh, you ought to have gone at once."

"I know. I was going as soon as Lucy left, but I thought I would attend to a little business down town first, and go to Mr. C——'s immediately on my return. When I came back, I thought I would look over the newspaper a little; I wanted to see what had been said in Congress on the tariff question, which is now the all-absorbing topic. I became so much interested in the remarks of one of the members, that I forgot all about Lucy Ellison until I was called off by a customer, who occupied me until dinner-time. But I will certainly attend to it this afternoon."

"Do, by all means. There should not be a moment's delay, for Mr. C——may supply himself with a teacher."

"Very true. If that were to happen through my neglect, I should never forgive myself."

"Hadn't you better call as you go to the store? It will be just in your way."

"So it will. Yes, I will call and put the matter in train at once," replied the husband.

With this good intention in his mind, Paul left his dwelling after dinner. He had only gone a couple of squares, however, before it occurred to him that as Mr. C——had only one session of his school, which let out at two or half-past two, he didn't know which, he of course did not dine before three o'clock, and as it was then just a quarter past three, it would not do to call upon him then; so he kept on to his store, fixing in his mind four o'clock as the hour at which he would call. Four o'clock found Paul deeply buried in a long series of calculations that were not completed for some time afterwards. On leaving his desk, he sat leisurely down in an arm-chair for the purpose of thinking about business. He had not thought long, before the image of Lucy Ellison came up before his mind. He drew out his watch.

"Nearly half-past four, I declare! I'm afraid Mr. C——is out now; but as it is so late, I will defer calling until I go home; it is just in my way. If I see him, I can drop in upon Mrs. Ellison after tea."

On his way home, Paul fell in with a friend whose conversation was very agreeable. He did not forget Lucy, but he thought a visit to Mr. C——would accomplish just as much after supper as before. So the call was deferred without a twinge of conscience.

The first words of Mrs. Burgess, on her husband's entrance, were, "Well, dear, what did Mr. C——say?"

"I haven't been able to see him yet, but I am going round after supper," Paul replied, quickly.

"Indeed! I am sorry. Did you call?"

"No; it occurred to me that C——dined at three o'clock, so I put it off until four."

"And didn't go then?"

"No; I was going to" —

"Yes, that is just like you, Paul!" spoke up his wife with some spirit, for she felt really provoked with her husband; "you are always *going to do!*"

"There, there," returned Paul, "don't say a word more. A few hours, one way or the other, can make no great difference. I will go round after tea and have the matter settled. I shall be much more likely to find C——in a state to talk about the matter than I would through the day."

As soon as tea was over, urged on by his wife, Paul put on his hat and started for the residence of Mr. C——. Unfortunately, that gentleman had gone out, and Paul turned away from his door much disappointed.

"I will call the first thing in the morning," he consoled himself by saying. "I will be sure to find him in then."

I am sorry to say that Paul was just going to do what he had promised Lucy he would do immediately, at least half-a-dozen times on the next day, but still failed in accomplishing his intended visit to Mr. C——. Mrs. Burgess scolded vigorously every time he came home, and he joined her in condemning himself, but still the thing had not been done when Paul laid his head that night rather uneasily upon his pillow.

When Lucy returned and related to her mother how kindly Mr. Burgess had received her, promising to call upon Mr. C——and secure the situation, if possible, the widow's heart felt warm with a grateful emotion. Light broke in upon her mind, that had been for a long time under a cloud.

"He was always a kind-hearted man," she said, "and ever ready to do a good deed. If he should be so fortunate as to obtain this place for you, we shall do very well; if not, heaven only knows what is to become of us."

"Do not give way to desponding thoughts, mother," returned Lucy; "all will yet be well. The vacancy has just occurred, and mine, I feel sure, will be the first application. Mr. Burgess's interest with Mr. C——, if he can be satisfied of my qualifications, must secure me the place."

"We ought to hear from him to-day," said Mrs. Ellison.

"Yes, I should think so. Mr. Burgess, of course, understands the necessity that always exists in a case of this kind for immediate application."

"Oh, yes, he'll do it all right. I feel perfectly willing to trust the matter in his hands."

As the reader has very naturally inferred, the circumstances of Mrs. Ellison were of rather a pressing nature. Her family consisted of three children, of whom Lucy was the eldest. Up to the time of her husband's death, she had been surrounded with every comfort she could desire; but Mr. Ellison's estate proving bankrupt, his family were left with but a small, and that a very uncertain income. Upon this, by the practice of great economy, they had managed to live. The final settlement of the estate took away this resource, and the widow found herself with only a small sum of money in hand, and all income cut off. This had occurred about a month before the period of Lucy's introduction to the reader. During this time, their gradually diminishing store, and the anxiety they felt in regard to the future, destroyed all the remains of former pride or regard for appearances, and made both Lucy and her mother willing to do any thing that would yield them an income, provided it were honourable. Nothing offered until nearly all their money was exhausted, and the minds of the mother and eldest daughter were in a state of great uncertainty and distress. Just at this darkest hour, intelligence of the vacancy in Mr. C——'s school reached their ears.

Such being their circumstances, it may well be supposed that Lucy and her mother felt deeply anxious to hear from Mr. Burgess, and counted not only the hours as they passed, but the minutes that made up the hours. Neither of them remarked on the fact that the day had nearly come to its close without any communication having been received, although both had expected to have heard much earlier from Mr. Burgess. As the twilight began to fall, its gloom making their hearts feel sadder, Mrs. Ellison said, "Don't you think we ought to have heard from Mr. Burgess by this time, Lucy?"

"I hoped to have received some intelligence before this," replied the daughter. "But perhaps we are impatient; it takes time to do every thing."

"Yes; but it wouldn't take Mr. Burgess long to call upon Mr. C— —. He might have done it in half an hour from the time you saw him."

"If he could have left his business to do so; but you know men in business cannot always command their time."

"I know; but still" —

"He has no doubt called," continued Lucy, interrupting her mother, for she could not bear to hear even an implied censure passed upon Mr. Burgess; "but he may not have obtained an interview with Mr. C— —, or he may be waiting for a definite answer. I think during the evening we shall certainly hear from him."

But notwithstanding Lucy and her mother lingered up until past eleven o'clock, the so-anxiously looked for communication was not received.

All the next day they passed in a state of nervous solicitude and anxious expectation, but night found them still ignorant as to what Mr. Burgess had done.

On the next day, unable to bear the suspense any longer, Lucy went to the store of Mr. Burgess about ten o'clock.

"Have you called upon Mr. C— —yet?" she asked, before he had time to more than bid her a good-morning.

"I was going to do it this moment," replied Mr. Burgess, looking confused, yet trying to assume a bland and cordial manner.

In spite of her efforts to appear indifferent, the countenance of Lucy fell and assumed a look of painful disappointment.

"You shall hear from me in an hour," said Mr. Burgess, feeling strongly condemned for his neglect. "I have had a great many things on my mind for these two days past, and have been much occupied with business. I regret exceedingly the delay, but you may rely upon my attending to it at once. As I said, I was just going out for the very purpose when you called. Excuse me to your mother, and tell her that she will certainly hear from me within the next hour. Tell her that I have already made one or two efforts to see Mr. C— —, but without succeeding in my object. He happened not to be at home when I called."

Lucy stammered out a reply, bade Mr. Burgess good-morning, and returned home with a heavy heart. She had little doubt but that the vacancy was already supplied. Scarcely half an hour elapsed, when a note was left. It was briefly as follows: —

"Mr. Burgess's compliments to Mrs. Ellison. Is very sorry to say that the vacancy in Mr. C— —'s seminary has already been filled. If in any thing else Mr. B. can be of any service, Mrs. E. will please feel at perfect liberty in calling upon him. He exceedingly regrets that his application to Mr. C— — was not more successful."

The note dropped from the hands of Mrs. Ellison, and she groaned audibly. Lucy snatched it up, and took in its contents at a single glance. She made no remark, but clasped her hands together and drew them tightly across her breast, while her eyes glanced involuntarily upward.

About an hour afterwards, a lady who felt a good deal of interest in Mrs. Ellison, and who knew of the application that was to be made through Mr. Burgess to Mr. C— —, called in to express her sincere regret at Lucy's having failed to secure the situation, a knowledge of which had just reached her ears.

"Nothing but the neglect of Mr. Burgess to call upon Mr. C— —at once, as he promised to do, has prevented Lucy from getting the place!" she said, with the warmth of a just indignation. "A person who was present when Mr. B. called this morning, told me, that after he left Mr. C— —remarked to her that he was perfectly aware of Lucy's high qualifications for teaching French, and would have been glad of her services had he known her wish to engage as an instructor, but that it was now too late, as he had on the day before employed a competent person to fill the situation."

Lucy covered her face with her hands on hearing this, and gave way to a passionate burst of tears.

When Mr. Burgess came home at dinner-time, his wife said, immediately on his entrance, "Have you secured that place for Lucy Ellison, my dear? I hope you haven't neglected it again."

"I called upon Mr. C— —this morning," replied the husband, "but found the vacancy already filled."

"Oh, I am so sorry!" said Mrs. Burgess, speaking in a tone of deep regret. "When was it filled?"

"I didn't inquire. Mr. C— —said that Lucy would have suited him exactly, but that her application came too late."

"Poor thing! She will be (sic) terrbly disappointed," said the wife.

"No doubt she will be disappointed, but I don't know why it should be so very terrible to her. She had no right to be positively certain of obtaining the situation."

"Have you heard any particulars of her mother's situation?" inquired Mrs. Burgess.

"Nothing very particular. Have you?"

"Yes. Mrs. Lemmon called to see me this morning; she is an intimate friend of Mrs. Ellison. She told me that the small income which Mrs. Ellison has enjoyed since her husband's death has, at the final settlement of his estate, been cut off, the estate proving to be utterly insolvent. A month has elapsed since she has been deprived of all means of living beyond the small sum of money that happened to be in her hands, an amount not over thirty or forty dollars. Since that time Lucy has been anxiously looking about for some kind of employment that would yield enough for the support of the family, to obtain which she was willing to devote every energy of body and mind. The vacancy in Mr. C— —'s school is the first opening of any kind that has yet presented itself. For this she was fully competent, and the salary would have supported the family quite comfortably. It is too bad that she should not have obtained it. I am almost sure, if you had gone at once to see about it, that you might have obtained it for her."

"Well, I was going to see about it at once, but something or other prevented me. If I really thought it was my fault, I should feel very bad."

That afternoon accident made him fully acquainted with the fact that he, and he alone, was to blame in the matter, and then he felt bad enough.

"That dreadful habit of procrastination," he murmured to himself, "is always getting me into trouble. If I alone were made to suffer, it would be no matter; but when it involves other people as it now does, it becomes a crime. In the present case I must make reparation in some way; but I must think how this is to be done."

When any matter serious enough to call for the undivided attention of Mr. Burgess presented itself, that thing was generally done, and well done. He had great energy of character, and mental resources beyond what were ordinarily possessed. It was only when he felt the want of an adequate purpose that neglect became apparent.

On the morning after the day upon which Lucy and her mother had been so bitterly disappointed, the former, while looking over the newspaper, called the attention of the latter to an advertisement of a young lady who was desirous of obtaining a situation as a French teacher in some private family or seminary. The advertiser represented herself as being thoroughly versed in the principles of the language, and able to speak it as well as a native of Paris. The highest testimonials as to character, education, social standing, &c. would be given.

"I think I had better do the same," Lucy said.

"It won't be of any use," replied the mother, in a tone of despondency.

"We don't know that, mother," said Lucy. "We must use the best means that offer themselves for the accomplishment of what we desire."

"There is already one advertisement for a situation such as you desire—some disappointed applicant for the place at Mr. C——'s, no doubt. It is hardly to be supposed that two more French teachers are wanted in the city."

"Let us try, mother," returned Lucy to this.

"If you feel disposed to do it, child, I have no objection," said Mrs. Ellison; "but I shall count nothing on it."

"It is the only method that now presents itself, and I think it will be right at least to make the trial. It can do no harm."

The more Lucy thought about an advertisement, the more hopeful did she feel about the result. During the day she prepared one and sent it down to a newspaper office. Her messenger had not been long gone before the servant came up to the room where she sat with her mother, and said that a gentleman was in the parlour and wished to see them. He had sent up his card.

"Mr. Burgess!" ejaculated Lucy, on taking the card from the servant's hand.

"I do not wish to see him," said Mrs. Ellison, as soon as the servant had withdrawn. "You will have to go down alone, Lucy."

Lucy descended to the parlour with reluctant steps, for she had little desire to see the man whose thoughtlessness and neglect had so cruelly wronged them. The moment she entered the parlour, Mr. Burgess stepped forward to meet her with a cheerful expression of countenance.

"Yesterday," he began immediately, "I had discouraging news for you, but I am happy to bring you a better story to-day. I have obtained a situation for you as a French teacher, in a new seminary which has just been opened, at a salary of six hundred dollars a year. If you will go with me immediately, I will introduce you to the principal, and settle all matters preliminary to your entering upon the duties of your station."

"I will be with you in a few minutes," was all that Lucy could say in reply, turning quickly away from Mr. Burgess and gliding from the room. Her heart was too full for her to trust herself to say more. In a moment after she was sobbing upon her mother's bosom. It was some minutes before she could command her feelings enough to tell the good news she had just heard. When she did find utterance, and briefly communicated the intelligence she had heard, her mother's tears of joy were mingled with her own.

Lucy accompanied Mr. Burgess to the residence of the principal of the new seminary, and there entered into a contract for one year to teach the French language, at a salary of six hundred dollars, her duties to commence at once, and her salary to be drawn weekly if she desired it. She did not attempt an expression of the gratitude that oppressed her bosom. Words would have been inadequate to convey her real feelings. But this was not needed. Mr. Burgess saw how deeply grateful she was, and wished for no utterance of what she felt.

That night both Mr. Burgess, as well as those he had benefited, had sweeter dreams than visited their pillows on the night preceding. The latter never knew how much they stood his debtor. He put in the advertisement which Lucy had read, and she was the person it described. Five hundred dollars was all the principal of the seminary paid; the other hundred was placed in his hands by Mr. Burgess, that the salary might be six hundred.

MAKING HASTE TO BE RICH.

"CENT to cent, shilling to shilling, and dollar to dollar, slowly and steadily, like the progress of a mole in the earth! That may suit some, but it will never do for Sidney Lawrence. There is a quicker road to fortune than that, and I am the man to walk in it. 'Enterprise' is the word. Yes, enterprise, enterprise, enterprise! Nothing venture, nothing gain, is my motto."

"Slow and sure is the safer motto, my young friend, and if you will take my advice, you will be content to creep before you walk, and to walk before you run. The cent to cent and dollar to dollar system is the only sure one."

This was the language of an old merchant, who had made his fortune by the system he recommended, and was addressed to a young man just entering business with a capital of ten thousand dollars, the joint property of himself and an only sister.

Sidney Lawrence had been raised in a large mercantile establishment, that was doing an immense business and making heavy profits. But all its operations were based upon adequate capital and enlarged experience. When he commenced for himself, he could not brook the idea of keeping near the shore, like a little boat, and following its safer windings; he felt like launching out boldly into the ocean and reaching the desired haven by the quickest course. He wished to accumulate money rapidly, and believed that, on the capital he possessed, five or six thousand dollars a year might as easily be made as one thousand, if a man only had sufficient enterprise to push business vigorously. The careful, plodding course pursued by some, and strongly recommended to him, he despised. It was beneath a man of true business capacity.

"As I said before, nothing venture, nothing gain," replied Lawrence to the old merchant's good advice. "I am not content to eke out a thousand or two dollars every year, and, at the age of fifty or sixty, retire from business on a paltry twenty or thirty thousand dollars. I must get rich fast, or not at all."

"Remember the words of Solomon, my young friend," returned the merchant. "'*He that maketh haste to be rich shall not be innocent.*' Among all the sayings of the wise man, there is not one truer than that. I have been in business for thirty years, and have seen the rise and fall of a good many 'enterprising' men, who were in a hurry to get rich. Their history is an instructive lesson to all who will read it. Some got rich, or at least appeared to get rich, in a very short space of time. They grew up like mushrooms in a night. But they were gone as quickly. I can point you to at least twenty elegant mansions, built by such men in their heyday of prosperity, that soon passed into other hands. And I can name to you half a dozen and more, who, when reverses came, were subjected to trials for alleged fraudulent practices, resorted to in extremity as a means of sustaining their tottering credit and escaping the ruin that threatened to engulf them. One of these, in particular, was a young man whom I raised, and who had always acted with the most scrupulous honesty while in my store. But he was ardent, ambitious, and anxious to get rich. His father started him in business with ten thousand dollars capital. In a little while, he was trading high, and pushing his business to the utmost of its capacity. At the end of a couple of years, his father had to advance him ten thousand dollars more to keep him from failing. During the next five years, he expanded with wonderful rapidity, built himself a splendid house, and took his place at the court end of the town, as one of our wealthy citizens. It was said of him that he had made a hundred thousand dollars. But the downfall came at last, as come I knew it must. He toppled over and fell down headlong. Then it was discovered that he had been making fictitious notes, purporting to be the bills payable of country merchants, which his own credit had carried through a number of the banks, as well as made pass freely to money-brokers. He had to stand a long and painful trial for forgery, and came within an ace of being sent to the State's prison. As soon as the trial closed, he left the city, and I have never heard of him since."

"But you don't mean to insinuate," said Lawrence, rather sternly, "that I would be guilty of forgery in any extremity?"

"Sidney Lawrence!" replied the merchant, speaking in a firm, serious voice, "I am a plain-spoken man, and always tell my real mind when I feel it my duty to do so, whether I give offence or not. That Solomon spoke truly, when he said, '*He that maketh haste to be rich shall not be innocent,*' I fully believe, because I am satisfied, from what I have seen and know of business, that whoever follows it with an eager desire to make money rapidly, will be subjected to daily temptations, and it will be almost impossible for him not to seek advantages over his neighbour in trade, and trample under foot the interests of others to gain his own. If this is done in little matters unscrupulously, it will in the end be done in great matters. What is the real difference, I should like to know, between taking advantage of a man in bargaining, and getting his money by passing upon him a forged note? The principle is undoubtedly the same, only one is a legal offence and the other is not. And therefore, I hold that he who takes an undue advantage of his fellow man in trade, will not in the end hesitate about committing a greater wrong, if he have a fair chance of escape from penalty. In my young days, the motto of most business men, who were not very nice about the interests of others, was, 'Every man for himself and the Lord for us all.' But the motto has become slightly changed in these times. It now reads, 'Every man for himself, and the d——l take the hindmost!' I hear this too often unblushingly avowed, but see it much oftener acted out, all around me. My young friend, if you wish to keep a clear conscience, adopt neither of these mottoes, but regard, in every transaction, the good of others as well as your own good. And let me most seriously and earnestly warn you against making haste to be rich. The least evil that can overtake you, in such an effort, will be the almost certain wreck of all your worldly hopes, some five or ten years hence, and your fall, so low, that to rise again will be almost impossible."

This well-meant, but plainly uttered advice, more than half offended Lawrence. He replied, coldly, that he thought he knew what he was about, and would try, at least, to "steer clear of the penitentiary."

With shrewdness, tact, untiring industry, and a spirit that knew no discouragement, the young man pressed forward in business. The warning of the merchant, if it did not repress his desire to get rich in haste, caused him to look more closely than he would otherwise have done into every transaction he was about to make. This saved him from many serious losses.

The want of more capital soon began to be felt. He saw good operations every day, that might be made if he had capital enough to enter into them.

"A man deserves no credit for getting rich, if he have capital enough to work with," was a favourite remark. "There is plenty of business to be done, and ways of making money in abundance, if the means are only at hand."

One week, if he had only been in the possession of means, he would have purchased a cotton-factory; the next week become possessor of a ship, and entered into the East India trade; and, the next week after that, purchased an interest in a lead-mine on the Upper Mississippi.

Money, money, more money, was ever his cry, for he saw golden opportunities constantly passing unimproved. A neighbour, to whom he was expressing his desire for the use of larger capital, said to him, one day—

"I'll tell you how you can get more money!"

"How?" was the eager question.

"Get into the direction of some bank, push through the notes of a business friend, in whom you have confidence, who will do the same for you in another bank of which he is one of the managers. There are wheels within wheels in those moneyed institutions, from which the few and not the many reap the most benefit. Connect yourself with as many as you can of them, and make the most of the opportunities such connections will afford. You know Balmier?"

"Yes."

"And what a rushing business he does?"

"Yes."

"He dragged heavily enough, and was always flying about for money, until he took a hint and got elected into the Citizens and Traders' Bank. Since then he has been as easy as an old shoe, and has done five times as much business as before."

"Is it possible?"

"Oh, yes! You are not fully up to the tricks of trade yet, I see, shrewd as you are."

"I know well enough how to use money, but I have not yet learned how to get it."

"That will all come in good time. We are just now getting up a petition for the charter of a new bank in which I am to be a director, and I can easily manage to get you in if you will subscribe pretty liberally to the stock. It is to be called the People's Bank."

"But I have no money to invest in stock. That would be taking away instead of adding to my capital in trade, which is light enough in all conscience."

"There will be no trouble about that. Only an instalment of twenty cents in the dollar will be necessary to set the institution going. And not more than ten cents in the dollar will be called in at a time. After two or three instalments have been paid, you can draw out two-thirds of the amount on stock notes."

"Indeed! That's the way it's done?"

"Yes. You ought to take about a hundred shares, which will make it easy for us to have you put into the Board of Directors."

"I'll do it," was the prompt response to this.

"And take my word for it, you will not be many months a bank director, if you improve the opportunities that will be thrown in your way, without having a good deal more money at your command than at present."

The charter for the People's Bank was obtained, and when an election was held, Lawrence went in as a director. He had not held that position many months, before, by favouring certain paper that was presented from certain quarters, he got paper favoured that came from certain other quarters; and in this was individually benefited by getting the use of about fifteen thousand dollars additional capital, which came to him really but not apparently from the bank in which he held a hundred shares of stock. For the sake of appearances, he did not borrow back his instalments on stock notes. It was a little matter, and would have looked as if he were pressed for money.

From this time Sidney Lawrence became a financier, and plunged deep into all the mysteries of money-raising. His business operations became daily more and more extended, and he never appeared to be much pressed for money. At the end of a couple of years, he held the office of director in two banking institutions, and was president of an insurance company that issued post-notes on which three per cent. was charged. These notes, as the institution was in good credit, could readily be passed through almost any bank in the city. They were loaned pretty freely on individual credit, and also freely on real estate and other collateral security.

It is hard to serve two masters. The mind of man is so constituted, and the influences bearing upon it are so peculiar in their orderly arrangements, that the more it is concentered upon one object and pursuit, the more perfection and certainty attend its action. But if it be divided between two objects and pursuits, and especially if both of these require much thought, its action will be imperfect to a certain degree in both, or one will suffer while the other absorbs the most attention.

Thus it happened with Lawrence. While ardently engaged in financiering, his business received less attention. Instead of using to the best possible advantage the money already obtained in his financiering operations, he strove eagerly after more. In fact, too reckless an investment, in many instances, of borrowed capital, from which no return could be obtained perhaps for years, made his wants still as great as before, and kept in constant activity all the resources of his mind in order to meet his accommodations and steadily to increase them.

Ten years from the time when Sidney Lawrence started in business have passed. He is living in handsome style and keeps his carriage. Five or six years previously, he was married to a beautiful and lovely-minded woman, connected with some of the best families of the city. He has three children.

"Are you not well, dear?" asked his wife, one day about this period. They were sitting at the dinner-table, and Mr. Lawrence was hardly tasting his food.

"I haven't much appetite," he replied indifferently.

"You eat scarcely any thing; hardly enough to keep you alive. I am afraid you give yourself too much up to business."

Mr. Lawrence did not reply. He had evidently not heard more than half of his wife's last remark. In a little while he left the table, saying, as he rose, that he had some business requiring his immediate attention. Mrs. Lawrence glanced toward the door that closed after her husband with a troubled look, and sighed.

From his dwelling Mr. Lawrence hurried to his store, and spent an hour there in examining his account books, and in making calculations. At five o'clock he met the directors of the insurance company, of which he was still president, at an extra meeting. All had grave faces. There was a statement of the affairs of the company upon the table around which they were gathered. It showed that in the next two weeks post-notes, amounting in all to one hundred and fifty thousand dollars, would fall due; while not over fifty thousand dollars in bills receivable, maturing within that time, were on hand, and the available cash resources of the company were not over five thousand dollars. The time was, when by an extra effort the sum needed could have been easily raised. But extra efforts had been put forth so often of late, that the company had exhausted nearly all its resources.

"I do not understand," remarked one of the directors, looking up from the statement he had been carefully examining, "how there can be a hundred and fifty thousand dollars of post-notes due so soon, and only fifty thousand dollars in bills receivable maturing in the same time. If I am not mistaken, the post-notes were never issued except against bills having a few days shorter time to run. How is this, Mr. Lawrence?"

"All that is plain enough," the president replied promptly. "A large portion of these bills have been at various times discounted for us in the People's Bank, and in other banks, when we have needed money."

"But why should we be in such need of money?" inquired the director earnestly. He had been half asleep in his place for over a year, and was just beginning to get his eyes open. "I believe we have had no serious losses of late. There have been but few fires that have touched us."

"But there have been a good many failures in the last six months, most of which have affected us, and some to quite a heavy amount," returned the president. "Our post-note business has proved most unfortunate."

"So I should think if it has lost us a hundred thousand dollars, as appears from this statement."

"It is useless to look at that now," said Mr. Lawrence. "The great business to be attended to is the raising of means to meet this trying emergency. How is it to be done?"

There was a deep silence and looks of concern.

"Can it be raised at all? Is there any hope of saving the institution?" asked one of the board, at length.

"In my opinion, none in the world," was replied by another. "I have thought of little else but the affairs of the company since yesterday, and I am satisfied that all hope is gone. There are thirty thousand dollars to be provided to-morrow. Our balance is but five thousand, even if all the bills maturing to-day have been paid."

"Which they have, I presume, as no protests have come in," remarked the president.

"But what is the sum of five thousand dollars set off against thirty thousand? It is as nothing."

"Surely, gentlemen are not prepared to give up in this way," said the president, earnestly. "A failure will be a most disastrous thing, and we shall all be deeply sufferers in the community if it takes place. We must make efforts and sacrifices to carry it through. Here are twelve of us; can we not, on our individual credit, raise the sum required? I, for one, will issue my notes to-morrow for twenty thousand dollars. If the other directors will come forward in the same spirit, we may exchange the bills among each other, and by endorsing them mutually, get them through the various banks where we have friends or influence, and thus save the institution. Gentlemen, are you prepared to meet me in this thing?"

Two or three responded affirmatively. Some positively declined; and others wanted time to think of it.

"If we pause to think, all is ruined," said Mr. Lawrence, excited. "We must act at once, and promptly."

But each member of the board remained firm to the first expression. Nothing could be forced, and reflection only tended to confirm those who opposed the president's views in their opposition to the plan suggested. The meeting closed, after two hours' perplexing deliberation, without determining upon any course of action. At ten o'clock on the next day the directors were to meet again.

Mr. Lawrence walked the floor for half of that night, and lay awake for the other half. To sleep was impossible. Thus far, in the many difficulties he had encountered, a way of escape from them had opened either on the right hand or on the left, but now no way of escape presented itself. A hundred plans were suggested to his mind, canvassed and then put aside. He saw but one measure of relief, if it could be carried out; but that he had proposed already, and it was not approved.

The unhappy state in which she saw her husband deeply distressed Mrs. Lawrence. Earnestly did she beg of him to tell her all that troubled him, and let her bear a part of the burden that was upon him. At first he evaded her questions; but, to her oft-repeated and tenderly urged petition to be a sharer in his pains as well as his pleasures, he mentioned the desperate state of affairs in the company of which he was president.

"But, my dear husband," she replied to this, "you cannot be held responsible for the losses the institution has sustained."

"True, Florence; but the odium, the censure, the distress that must follow its failure,—I cannot bear to think of these. My credit, too, will suffer, for I shall lose all I have invested in the stock, and this fact, when known, will impair confidence."

"All this is painful and deeply to be regretted, Sidney," said the wife, speaking in as firm a voice as she could assume. "But as it is a calamity that cannot now be avoided, and is not the result of any wrong act of yours, let a clear conscience sustain you in this severe trial. Let the public censure, let odium be attached to your name—so long as your conscience is clear and your integrity unsullied, these cannot really hurt you."

But this appeal had little or no effect. The mind of the unhappy man could not take hold of it, nor feel its force. It was repeated again and again, and with as little effect. Finally he begged to be left to his own reflections. In tears his wife complied with his request. That night she slept as little as her miserable husband.

On the next day the——Insurance Company was dishonoured, and "went into liquidation." On the day following Sidney Lawrence suspended payment. Trustees were appointed to take charge of the effects of the company, who immediately commenced a rigid examination into its affairs. Lawrence made an assignment at the same time for the benefit of his creditors.

One evening, about a week after his failure, Mr. Lawrence came home paler and more disturbed than ever. There was something wild in the expression of his countenance.

"Florence," said he, as soon as he was alone with her, "I must leave for Cincinnati in the morning."

"Why?" eagerly asked the wife, her face instantly blanching.

"Business requires me to go. I have seen your father, and have made arrangements with him for you to go to his house, with the children, while I am away. This property, as I have before told you, has to be sold, and the sale will probably take place while I am gone."

"How soon will you return?"

"I cannot tell exactly; but I will come back as quickly as possible."

There was something in the manner of her husband, as he made this announcement, that startled and alarmed Mrs. Lawrence. She tried to ask many questions, but her voice failed her. Leaning her head down upon her husband's breast, she sobbed and wept for a long time. Lawrence was much affected, and kissed the wet cheek of his wife with unwonted fervour.

On the next morning, early, the unhappy man parted with his family. His wife clung to him with an instinctive dread of the separation. Tears were in his eyes, as he took his children one after another in his arms and kissed them tenderly.

"God bless you all, and grant that we may meet again right early, and under brighter skies!" he said, as he clasped his wife to his bosom in a long embrace, and then tore himself away.

On the third day after Mr. Lawrence left, one of the city newspapers contained the following paragraph:

"THE— —INSURANCE COMPANY.—We understand that in the investigation of the affairs of this concern, it has been discovered that Mr. Lawrence, the president, proves to be a defaulter in the sum of nearly a hundred thousand dollars. The public are aware that post-notes were issued by the company to a large amount, and loaned to individuals on good collateral security. These bore only the signature of the president. It now appears that Mr. Lawrence used this paper without the knowledge of the directors. He signed what he wanted for his own use, and when these came due, signed others and negotiated them, managing through the principal clerk in the institution, who it seems was an accomplice, to keep the whole matter a secret. This was continued until he had used the credit of the concern up to a hundred thousand dollars, when it sank under the load. Preparations were made, immediately on the discovery of this, to have him arrested and tried for swindling, but he got wind of it and has left the city. We presume, however, that he will be apprehended and brought back. His own private affairs are said to be in a most deplorable condition. It is thought that not over twenty cents in the dollar will be realized at the final settlement."

Here we drop a veil over the history of the man who made haste to be rich, and was not innocent. His poor wife waited vainly for him to return, and his children asked often for their father, and wondered why he stayed so long away. Years passed before they again met, and then it was in sorrow and deep humiliation.

LET HER POUT IT OUT.

I HOPE there is no coolness between you and Maria," said Mrs. Appleton to her young friend, Louisa Graham, one evening at a social party. "I have not seen you together once to-night; and just now she passed without speaking, or even looking at you."

"Oh, as to that," replied Louisa, tossing her head with an air of contempt and affected indifference, "she's got into a pet about something; dear knows what, for I don't."

"I am really sorry to hear you say so," remarked Mrs. Appleton. "Maria is a warm-hearted girl, and a sincere friend. Why do you not go to her, and inquire the cause of this change in her manner?"

"Me! No, indeed. I never humour any one who gets into a pet and goes pouting about in that manner."

"But is it right for you to act so? A word of inquiry or explanation might restore all in a moment."

"Right or wrong, I never did and never will humour the whims of such kind of people. No, no. Let her pout it out! That's the way to cure such people."

"I don't think so, Louisa. She is unhappy from some real or imaginary cause. That cause it is no doubt in your power to remove."

"But she has no right to imagine causes of offence; and I don't choose to have people act as she is now acting towards me from mere imaginary causes. No; let her pout it out, I say. It will teach her a good lesson."

Louisa spoke with indignant warmth.

"Were you never mistaken?" asked Mrs. Appleton, in a grave tone.

"Of course, I've been mistaken many a time."

"Very well. Have you never been mistaken in reference to another's action towards you?"

"I presume so."

"And have not such mistakes sometimes given you pain?"

"I cannot recall any instances just at this moment, but I have no doubt they have."

"Very well. Just imagine yourself in Maria's position; would you not think it kind in any one to step forward and disabuse you of an error that was stealing away your peace of mind?"

"Yes; but, Mrs. Appleton, I don't know anything about the cause of Maria's strange conduct. She may see that in my character or disposition to which she is altogether uncongenial, and may have made up her mind not to keep my company any longer. Or she may feel herself, all at once, above me. And I'm not the one, I can tell you, to cringe to any living mortal. I am as good as she is, or any one else!"

"Gently, gently, Louisa! Don't fall into the very fault you condemn in Maria; that of imagining a sentiment to be entertained by another which she does not hold, and then growing indignant over the idea and at the person supposed to hold it."

"I can't see clearly the force of what you say, Mrs. Appleton; and therefore I must come back to what I remarked a little while ago: She must pout it out."

"You are wrong, Louisa," her friend replied, "and I cannot let you rest in that wrong, if it is in my power to correct it. Perhaps, by relating a circumstance that occurred with myself a few years ago, I may be able to make an impression on your mind. I had, and still have, an esteemed friend, amiable and sincere, but extremely sensitive. She is too apt to make mistakes about other people's estimation of her, which, I often told her, is a decided fault of character. That she has only to be self-conscious of integrity, and then she will be truly estimated. Well, this friend would sometimes imagine that *I* treated her coolly, or indifferently, or thrust at her feelings, when I felt towards her all the while a very warm affection. The consequence would be, that she would assume a cold or offended exterior. But I never said to myself, 'Let her pout it out.' I knew that she was mistaken, and that she was really suffering under her mistake; and I would always go to her, and kindly inquire the cause of her changed manner. The result was, of course, an immediate restoration of good feeling, often accompanied by a confession of regret at having injured me by imagining that I entertained unkind sentiments when I did not. On one occasion I noticed a kind of reserve in her manner; but thinking there might be some circumstances known only to herself, that gave her trouble, I did not seem to observe it. On the next morning I was exceedingly pained and surprised to receive a note from her, in something like the following language—

"The fact is, Mrs. Appleton, I cannot and will not bear any longer your manner towards me. You seem to think that I have no feelings. And besides, you assume an air of superiority and patronage that is exceedingly annoying. Last night your manner was insufferable. As I have just said, I cannot and will not bear such an assumption on your part. And now let me say, that I wish, hereafter, to be considered by you as a stranger. As such I shall treat you. Do not attempt to answer this, do not attempt to see me, for I wish for no humiliating explanations.'

"Now what would you have done in such a case, Louisa?"

"I would have taken her at her word, of course," was the prompt reply; "did not you?"

"Oh, no; that would not have been right."

"I must confess, Mrs. Appleton, that your ideas of right, and mine, are very different. This lady told you expressly that she did not wish to hold any further intercourse with you."

"Exactly. But, then, she would not have said so, had she not been deceived by an erroneous idea. Knowing this, it became my duty to endeavour to remove the false impression."

"I must confess, Mrs. Appleton, that I cannot see it in the same light. I don't believe that we are called upon to humour the whims of every one. It does such people, as you speak of, good to be let alone, and have their pout out. If you notice them, it makes them ten times as bad."

"A broad assertion like that you have just made needs proof, Louisa. I, for one, do not believe that it is true. If an individual, under a false impression, be let alone to 'pout it out,' the mere pouting, as you call it, does not bring a conviction that the cause of unpleasant feeling is altogether imaginary. The ebullition will subside in time, and the subject of it may seem to forget the cause; but to do so, is next to impossible where the false impression is not removed. Now let me tell you how *I* did in reference to the friend I have just mentioned."

"Well. How did you do?"

"After the acute pain of mind which was caused by her note had subsided, I began to examine, as far as I could recollect them, all my words and actions towards her on the previous evening. In one or two things, I thought I could perceive that which to one of her sensitive disposition might appear in a wrong light. I remembered, too, that in her domestic relations there were some circumstances of a painful character, and I knew that these weighed heavily upon her mind, often depressing her spirits very much. One of these circumstances, though perfectly beyond her control, was extremely humiliating to a high-minded and somewhat proud-spirited woman. All these things I turned over in my mind, and instead of suffering myself to feel incensed against her for the unkind note she had written to me, I endeavoured to find excuses for her, and to palliate her fault all that I could. What troubled me most, was the almost insurmountable barrier that she had thrown between us. 'Do not attempt to answer this; do not attempt to see me;' were strong positions; and my pride rose up, and forbade me to break through them. But pride could not stand before the awakening of better feelings. 'I must see her. I will see her!' I said.

"This resolution taken, I determined that I would not call upon her until towards evening, thus giving her time for reflection. The hour at length came in which I had made up my mind to perform a most painful duty, and I dressed myself for the trying visit. When I pulled the bell, on pausing at her door, I was externally calm, but internally agitated.

"'Tell Mrs.— —that a friend wishes to speak to her,' said I to the servant who showed me into the parlour. I did not feel at liberty to ask her not to mention my name; but I emphasized the word 'friend,' in hopes that she would understand my meaning. But she either did not or would not, for in a few minutes she returned and said, in a confused and hesitating voice,
"'Mrs.—says that she does not wish to see you.'"

"And you left the house on the instant?" Louisa said, in an indignant tone.

"No, I did not," was Mrs. Appleton's calm reply.

"Not after such an insult! Pardon me—but I should call it a breach of politeness for any one to remain in the house of another under such circumstances."

"But, Louisa, you must remember that there are exceptions to every general rule; and also, that the same act may be good or bad, according to the end which the actor has in view. If I had proposed to myself any mere sinister and selfish end in remaining in the house of my friend after such an unkind and to me, at the time, cruel repulse, I should have acted wrong; but my end was to benefit my friend—to disabuse her of a most painful mistake, which I could only do by meeting her, and letting her ears take in the tones of my voice, that she might thus judge of my sincerity."

Louisa did not reply, and Mrs. Appleton continued,—

"'Tell Mrs.——,' said I to the servant, 'that I am very anxious to see her, and that she must not refuse me an interview.' In a few minutes she returned with the positive refusal of Mrs.——to see me. There was one thing that I did not want to do—one thing that I hesitated to do, and that was to force myself upon my estranged friend by intruding upon her, even in her own chamber, where she had retired to be secure from my importunity. But I looked to the end I had in view. 'Is not the end a good one?' I said, as I mused over the unpleasant position in which I found myself. 'Will not even Mrs.—— thank me for the act after she shall have perceived her error?' Thus I argued with myself, and finally made up my mind that I would compel an interview by entering my friend's chamber, even though she had twice refused to see me.

"As I resolved to do, so I acted. Once fully convinced that the act was right, I compelled myself to do it, without once hesitating or looking back. My low knock at her chamber-door was unanswered. I paused but a few moments before opening it. There stood my friend, with a pale yet firm countenance, and as I advanced she looked me steadily in the face with a cold, repulsive expression.

"'Mrs.— —,' said I, extending my hand and forcing a smile, while the tears came to my eyes, and my voice trembled—'if I had been guilty of the feelings with which you have charged me, I would not have thus sought you, in spite of all your repulses. Let me now declare to you, in the earnestness of a sincere heart, that I am innocent of all you allege against me. I have always regarded you as one of my choicest friends. I have always endeavoured to prefer you before myself, instead of setting myself above you. You have, therefore, accused me wrongfully, but I do most heartily forgive you. Will you not then forgive me for an imaginary fault?'

"For a few moments after I commenced speaking, she continued to look at me with the same cold, repulsive stare, not deigning to touch the hand that I still extended. But she saw that I was sincere; she felt that I was sincere, and this melted her down. As I ceased speaking, she started forward with a quick, convulsed movement, and throwing her arms around me, hid her face in my bosom and wept aloud. It was some time before the tumult of her feelings subsided.

"'Can you indeed forgive me?' she at length said; 'my strange, blind, wayward folly?'

"'Let us be friends as we were, Mrs.— —,' I replied, 'and let this hour be forgotten, or only remembered as a seal to our friendship.'

"From that day, Louisa, there has been no jarring string in our friendly intercourse. Mrs.— —really felt aggrieved; she thought that she perceived in my conduct all that she had alleged, and it wounded her to the quick. But the earnest sincerity with which I sought her out and persisted in seeing her, convinced her that she had altogether misunderstood the import of my manner, which, under the peculiar state of her feelings, put on a false appearance."

"Well, Mrs. Appleton," Louisa said with a deep inspiration, as that lady ceased speaking, "I cannot say that I think you did wrong: indeed, I feel that you were right; but I cannot act from such unselfish motives; it is not in me."

"But you can compel yourself to do right, Louisa, even where there is no genuine good impulse prompting to correct actions. It is by our thus compelling ourselves, and struggling against the activity of a wrong motive, that a right one is formed. If I had consulted only my feelings, and had suffered only offended self-love to speak, I should never have persevered in seeing my friend; to this day there would have been a gulf between us."

"Still, it seems to me that we ought not, as a general thing, to humour persons in these idle whims; it only confirms them in habits of mind that make them sources of perpetual annoyance to their friends. Indeed, as far as I am concerned, I desire to be freed from acquaintances of this description; I do not wish my peace ever and anon interfered with in such an unpleasant way."

"We should not," Mrs. Appleton replied, "consider only ourselves in these, or indeed in any matters pertaining to social intercourse, but should endeavour sometimes to look away from what is most pleasant and gratifying to ourselves, and study to make others happy. You know that the appearance which true politeness puts on is that of preferring others to ourselves. We offer them the best seats, or the most eligible positions; or present them with the choicest viands at the table. We introduce subjects of conversation that we think will interest others more than ourselves, and deny ourselves in various ways, that others may be obliged and gratified. Now, the question is, are these mere idle and unmeaning forms? Or is it right that we should feel as we act? If they are unmeaning forms, then are the courtesies of social intercourse a series of acts most grossly hypocritical. If not so, then it is right that we should prefer others to ourselves; and it is right for us, when we find that a friend is under a painful mistake—even if to approach her may cause some sacrifice of our feelings—for us to go to that friend and disabuse her mind of error. Do you not think so, Louisa?"

"I certainly cannot gainsay your position, Mrs. Appleton; but still I feel altogether disinclined to make any overtures to Maria."

"Why so, Louisa?"

"Because I can imagine no cause for her present strange conduct, and therefore see no way of approaching"—

The individual about whom they had been conversing passed near them at this moment, and caused Mrs. Appleton and Louisa to remember that they were prolonging their conversation to too great an extent for a social party.

"We will talk about this again," Mrs. Appleton said, rising and passing to the side of Maria.

"You do not seem cheerful to-night, Maria; or am I mistaken in my observation of your face?" Mrs. Appleton said in a pleasant tone.

"I was not aware that there was any thing in my manner that indicated the condition of mind to which you allude," the young lady replied, with a smile.

"There seemed to me such an indication, but perhaps it was only an appearance."

"Perhaps so," said Maria, with something of abstraction in her manner. A silence, embarrassing in some degree to both parties, followed, which was broken by an allusion of Mrs. Appleton's to Louisa Graham.

To this, Maria made no answer.

"Louisa is a girl of kind feelings," remarked Mrs. Appleton.

"She is so esteemed," Maria replied, somewhat coldly.

"Do you not think so, Maria?"

"Why should I think otherwise?"

"I am sure I cannot tell; but I thought there was something in your manner that seemed to indicate a different sentiment."

To this the young lady made no reply, and Mrs. Appleton did not feel at liberty to press the subject, more particularly as she wished to induce Louisa, if she could possibly do so, to sacrifice her feelings and go to Maria with an inquiry as to the cause of her changed manner. She now observed closely the manner of Maria, and saw that she studiously avoided coming into contact with Louisa. Thus the evening passed away, and the two young ladies retired without having once spoken to each other.

Unlike too many of us under similar circumstances, Mrs. Appleton did not say within herself, "This is none of my business. If they have fallen out, let them make it up again." Or, "If she chooses to get the 'pouts' for nothing, let her pout it out." But she thought seriously about devising some plan to bring about explanations and a good understanding again between two who had no just cause for not regarding each other as friends. It would have been an easy matter to have gone to Maria and to have asked the cause of her changed manner towards Louisa, and thus have brought about a reconciliation; but she was desirous to correct a fault in both, and therefore resolved, if possible, to induce the latter to go to the former. With this object in view, she called upon Louisa early on the next morning.

"I was sorry to see," she said, after a brief conversation on general topics, "that there was no movement on the part of either yourself or Maria to bring about a mutual good understanding."

"I am sure, Mrs. Appleton, that I haven't any thing to do in the matter," was Louisa's answer. "I have done nothing wilfully to wound or offend Maria, and therefore have no apologies to make. If she sees in my character any thing so exceedingly offensive as to cause her thus to recede from me, I am sure that I do not wish her to have any kind of intercourse with me."

"That is altogether out of the question, Louisa. Maria has seen nothing real in you at which to be offended; it is an imaginary something that has blinded her mind."

"In that case, Mrs. Appleton, I must say, as I said at first—Let her pout it out. I have no patience with any one who acts so foolishly."

"You must pardon my importunity, Louisa," her persevering friend replied. "I am conscious that the position you have taken is a wrong one, and I cannot but hope that I shall be able to make you see it."

"I don't know, Mrs. Appleton; none are so blind, it is said, as they who will not see," Louisa replied, with a meaning smile.

"So you are conscious of an unwillingness to see the truth if opposed to your present feelings," said Mrs. Appleton, smiling in return; "I have some hope of you now."

"You think so?"

"Oh, yes; the better principles of your mind are becoming more active, and I now feel certain that you will think of Maria as unhappy from some erroneous idea which it is in your power to remove."

"But her unkind and ungenerous conduct towards me" —

"Don't think of that, Louisa; think only if it be not in your power again to restore peace to her mind; again to cause her eyes to brighten and her lips to smile when you meet her. It is in your power—I know that it is. Do not, then, let me beg of you, abuse that power, and suffer one heart to be oppressed when a word from you can remove the burden that weighs it down."

To this appeal Laura remained silent for a few moments, and then looking up, said, "What would you have me do, Mrs. Appleton?"

"Nothing but what you see to be clearly right. Do not act simply from my persuasion. I urge you as I do, that you may perceive it to be a duty to go to Maria and try to disabuse her of an error that is producing unhappiness."

"Then how do you think I ought to act?"

"It seems to me that you should go to Maria, and ask her, with that sincerity and frankness that she could not mistake, the cause of her changed manner; and that you should, at the same time, say that you were altogether unconscious of having said or done any thing to wound or offend her."

"I will do it, Mrs. Appleton," said Louisa, after musing for a few moments.

"But does it seem to you right that you should do so?"

"It does when I lose sight of myself, and think of Maria as standing to another in the same light that she really stands to me."

"I am glad that you have thus separated your own feelings from the matter; that is the true way to view every subject that has regard to our actions towards others. Go, then, to your estranged friend on this mission of peace, and I know that the result will be pleasant to both of you."

"I am fully convinced that it is right for me to do so; and more, I am fully resolved to do what I see to be right."

About an hour after the closing of this interview, Louisa called at the house of her friend. It was some minutes after she had sent up her name before Maria descended to the parlour to meet her. As she came in she smiled a faint welcome, extending at the same time her hand in a cold formal manner. Louisa was chilled at this, for her feelings were quick; but she suppressed every weakness with an effort, and said, as she still held the offered hand within her own—

"There must be something wrong, Maria, or *you* would never treat me so coldly. As I am altogether unconscious of having said or done any thing to wound your feelings, or injure you in any way, I have felt constrained to come and see you, and ask if in any thing I have unconsciously done you an injury."

There was a pause of some moments, during which Maria was evidently endeavouring to quiet her thoughts and feelings, so as to give a coherent and rational response to what had been said; but this she was unable to do.

"I am a weak and foolish girl, Louisa," she at length said, as the moisture suffused her eyes; "and now I am conscious that I have wronged you. Let us forget the past, and again be friends as we were."

"I am still your friend, Maria, and still wish to remain your friend; but in order that, hereafter, there may be no further breach of this friendship, would it not be well for you to tell me, frankly, in what manner I have wounded your feelings?"

"Perhaps so; but still I would rather not tell the cause; it involves a subject upon which I do not wish to speak. Be satisfied, then, Louisa, that I am fully convinced that you did not mean to wound me. Let this (kissing her tenderly) assure you that my old feelings have all returned. But do not press me upon a point that I shrink from even thinking about."

There was something so serious, almost solemn in the manner of the young lady, that Louisa felt that it would be wrong to urge her upon the subject. But their reconciliation was complete.

So much interest did Mrs. Appleton feel in the matter, that she called in, during the afternoon of the same day, to see Louisa.

"Well, it's all made up," was almost the first word uttered as Mrs. Appleton came in.

"I am truly glad to hear it," replied that lady.

"And I am glad to be able to say so; but there is one thing that I do not like: I could not prevail upon her to tell me the cause of her coldness towards me."

"I am sorry for that, because, not knowing what has given offence, you are all the time liable again to trespass on feelings that you desire not to wound."

"So I feel about it; but the subject seemed so painful to her that I did not press it."

"When did you first notice a change in her manner?"

"About a week ago, when we were spending an evening at Mrs. Trueman's."

"Cannot you remember something which you then said that might have wounded her?"

"No, I believe not. I have tried several times to recall what I then said, but I can think of nothing but a light jest which I passed upon her about her certainly coming of a crazy family."

"Surely you did not say that, Louisa!"

"Yes, I did. And I am sure that I thought no harm of it. We were conversing gayly, and she was uttering some of her peculiar, and often strange sentiments, when I made the thoughtless and innocent remark I have alluded to. No one replied, and there was a momentary silence that seemed to me strange. From that time her manner changed. But I have never believed that my playful remark was the cause. I think her a girl of too much good sense for that."

"Have you never heard that her father was for many years in the hospital, and at last died there a raving maniac?" asked Mrs. Appleton with a serious countenance.

"Never," was the positive answer.

"It is true that such was his miserable end, Louisa."

"Then it is all explained. Oh, how deeply I must have wounded her!"

"Deeply, no doubt. But it cannot be helped. The wound, I trust, is now nearly healed." Then, after a pause, Mrs. Appleton resumed:

"Let this lesson never be forgotten, my young friend. Suppose you had followed your own impulses, and let Maria 'pout it out,' as you said; how much would both she and yourself have suffered—she, under the feeling that you had wantonly insulted and wounded her; and you, in estranged friendship, and under the imputation, unknown to yourself, of having most grossly violated the very first principles of humanity. Let the lesson, then, sink deeply into your heart. Never again permit any one to grow cold towards you suddenly, without inquiring the cause. It is due to yourself and your friends."

"I shall never forget the lesson, Mrs. Appleton," was Louisa's emphatic response.

"A FINE, GENEROUS FELLOW."

MY friend Peyton was what is called a "fine, generous fellow." He valued money only as a means of obtaining what he desired, and was always ready to spend it with an acquaintance for mutual gratification. Of course, he was a general favourite. Every one spoke well of him, and few hesitated to give his ears the benefit of their good opinion. I was first introduced to him when he was in the neighbourhood of twenty-two years of age. Peyton was then a clerk in the receipt of six hundred dollars a year. He grasped my hand with an air of frankness and sincerity, that at once installed him in my good opinion. A little pleasure excursion was upon the tapis, and he insisted upon my joining it. I readily consented. There were five of us, and the expense to each, if borne mutually, would have been something like one dollar. Peyton managed every thing, even to paying the bills; and when I offered to repay him my proportion, he said —

"No, no!" — pushing back my hand — "nonsense!"

"Yes; but I must insist upon meeting my share of the expense."

"Not a word more. The bill's settled, and you needn't trouble your head about it," was his reply; and he seemed half offended when I still urged upon him to take my portion of the cost.

"What a fine, generous fellow Peyton is!" said one of the party to me, as we met on the next day.

"Did he also refuse to let you share in the expense of our excursion?" I asked.

"After what he said to you, I was afraid of offending him by proposing to do so."

"He certainly is generous—but, I think, to a fault, if I saw a fair specimen of his generosity yesterday."

"We should be just, as well as generous."

"I never heard that he was not just."

"Nor I. But I think he was not just to himself. And I believe it will be found to appear in the end, that, if we are not just to ourselves, we will, somewhere in life, prove unjust to others. I think that his salary is not over twelve dollars a week. If he bore the whole expense of our pleasure excursion, it cost him within a fraction of half his earnings for a week. Had we all shared alike, it would not have been a serious matter to either of us."

"Oh! as to that, it is no very serious matter to him. He will never think of it."

"But, if he does so very frequently, he may feel it sooner or later," I replied.

"I'm sure I don't know any thing about that," was returned. "He is a generous fellow, and I cannot but like him. Indeed, every one likes him."

A few evenings afterwards I met Peyton again.

"Come, let us have some oysters," said he.

I did not object. We went to an oyster-house, and ate and drank as much as our appetites craved. He paid the bill!

Same days afterwards, I fell in with him again, and, in order to retaliate a little, invited him to go and get some refreshments with me. He consented. When I put my hand in my pocket to pay for them, his hand went into his. But I was too quick for him. He seemed uneasy about it. He could feel pleased while giving, but it evidently worried him to be the recipient.

From that time, for some years, I was intimate with the young man. I found that he set no true value upon money. He spent it freely with every one; and every one spoke well of him. "What a generous, whole-souled fellow he is!" or, "What a noble heart he has!" were the expressions constantly made in regard to him. While "Mean fellow!" "Miserly dog!" and other such epithets, were unsparingly used in speaking of a quiet, thoughtful young man, named Merwin, who was clerk with him in the same store. Merwin appeared to set an undue value upon money. He rarely indulged himself in any way, and it was with difficulty that he could ever be induced to join in any pleasures that involved expense. But I always observed that when he did so, he was exact about paying his proportion.

About two years after my acquaintance with Peyton began, an incident let me deeper into the character and quality of his generosity. I called one day at the house of a poor widow woman who washed for me, to ask her to do up some clothes, extra to the usual weekly washing. I thought she looked as if she were in trouble about something, and said so to her.

"It's very hard, at best," she replied, "for a poor woman, with three or four children to provide for, to get along—especially if, like me, she has to depend upon washing and ironing for a living. But when so many neglect to pay her regularly" —

"Neglect to pay their washerwoman!" I said, in a tone of surprise, interrupting her.

"Oh, yes. Many do that!"

"Who?"

"Dashing young men, who spend their money freely, are too apt to neglect these little matters, as they call them."

"And do young men, for whom you work, really neglect to pay you?"

"Some do. There are at least fifteen dollars now owed to me, and I don't know which way to turn to get my last month's rent for my landlord, who has been after me three times this week already. Mr. Peyton owes me ten dollars, and I can't" —

"Mr. Peyton? It can't be possible!"

"Yes, it is, though. He used to be one of the most punctual young men I washed for. But, of late, he never has any money."

"He's a very generous-hearted young man."

"Yes, I know he is," she replied. "But something is wrong with him. He looks worried whenever I ask him for money; and sometimes speaks as if half angry with me for troubling him. There's Mr. Merwin—I wish all were like him. I have never yet taken home his clothes, that I didn't find the money waiting for me, exact to a cent. He counts every piece when he lays out his washing for me, and knows exactly what it will come to: and then, if he happens to be out, the change is always left with the chambermaid. It's a pleasure to do any thing for him."

"He isn't liked generally as well as Mr. Peyton is," said I.

"Isn't he? It's strange!" the poor woman returned, innocently.

On the very next day, I saw Peyton riding out with an acquaintance in a buggy.

"Who paid for your ride, yesterday?" I said to the latter, with whom I was quite familiar, when next we met.

"Oh, Peyton, of course. He always pays, you know. He's a fine, generous fellow. I wish there were more like him."

"That you might ride out for nothing a little oftener, hey?"

My friend coloured slightly.

"No, not that," said he. "But you know there is so much selfishness in the world; we hardly ever meet a man who is willing to make the slightest sacrifice for the good of others."

"True. And I suppose it is this very selfishness that makes us so warmly admire a man like Mr. Peyton, who is willing to gratify us at his own charge. It's a pleasant thing to ride out and see the country, but we are apt to think twice about the costs before we act once. But if some friend will only stand the expense, how generous and whole-souled we think him! It is the same in every thing else. We like the enjoyments, but can't afford the expense; and he is a generous, fine-hearted fellow, who will squander his money in order to gratify us. Isn't that it, my friend?" said I, slapping him on the shoulder.

He looked half convinced, and a little sheepish, to use an expressive Saxonism.

On the evening succeeding this day, Peyton sat alone in his room, his head leaning upon his hand, and his brow contracted. There was a tap at his door. "Come in." A poorly-clad, middle-aged woman entered. It was his washerwoman.

The lines on the young man's brow became deeper.

"Can't you let me have some money, Mr. Peyton? My landlord is pressing hard for his rent, and I cannot pay him until you pay me."

"Really, Mrs. Lee, it is impossible just now; I am entirely out of money. But my salary will be due in three weeks, and then I will pay you up the whole. You must make your landlord wait until that time. I am very sorry to put you to this trouble. But it will never happen again."

The young man really did feel sorry, and expressed it in his face as well as in the tone of his voice.

"Can't you let me have one or two dollars, Mr. Peyton? I am entirely out of money."

"It is impossible—I haven't a shilling left. But try and wait three weeks, and then it will all come to you in a lump, and do you a great deal more good than if you had it a dollar at a time."

Mrs. Lee retired slowly, and with a disappointed air. The young man sighed heavily as she closed the door after her. He had been too generous, and now he could not be just. The buggy in which he had driven out with his friend on that day had cost him his last two dollars—a sum which would have lightened the heart of his poor washerwoman.

"The fact is, my salary is too small," said he, rising and walking about his room uneasily. "It is not enough to support me. If the account were fully made up, tailor's bill, bootmaker's bill, and all, I dare say I should find myself at least three hundred dollars in debt."

Merwin received the same salary that he did, and was just three hundred dollars ahead. He dressed as well, owed no man a dollar, and was far happier. It is true, he was not called a "fine, generous fellow," by persons who took good care of their own money, while they were very willing to enjoy the good things of life at a friend's expense. But he did not mind this. The want of such a reputation did not disturb his mind very seriously.

After Mrs. Lee had been gone half an hour, Peyton's door was flung suddenly open. A young man, bounding in, with extended hand came bustling up to him.

"Ah, Peyton, my fine fellow! How are you? how are you?" And he shook Peyton's hand quite vigorously.

"Hearty!—and how are you, Freeman?"

"Oh, gay as a lark. I have come to ask a favour of you."

"Name it."

"I want fifty dollars."

Peyton shrugged his shoulders.

"I must have it, my boy! I never yet knew you to desert a friend, and I don't believe you will do so now."

"Suppose I haven't fifty dollars?"

"You can borrow it for me. I only want it for a few days. You shall have it back on next Monday. Try for me—there's a generous fellow!"

"There's a generous fellow," was irresistible. It came home to Peyton in the right place. He forgot poor Mrs. Lee, his unpaid tailor's bill, and sundry other troublesome accounts.

"If I can get an advance of fifty dollars on my salary to-morrow, you shall have it."

"Thank you! thank you! I knew I shouldn't have to ask twice when I called upon Henry Peyton. It always does me good to grasp the hand of such a man as you are."

On the next day, an advance of fifty dollars was asked and obtained. This sum was loaned as promised. In two weeks, the individual who borrowed it was in New Orleans, from whence he had the best of reasons for not wishing to return to the north. Of course, the generous Henry Peyton lost his money.

An increase of salary to a thousand dollars only made him less careful of his money. Before, he lived as freely as if his income had been one-third above what it was; now, he increased his expenses in a like ratio. It was a pleasure to him to spend his money—not for himself alone, but among his friends.

It is no cause of wonder, that in being so generous to some, he was forced to be unjust to others. He was still behindhand with his poor old washer-woman—owed for boarding, clothes, hats, boots, and a dozen other matters—and was, in consequence, a good deal harassed with duns. Still, he was called by some of his old cronies, "a fine, generous fellow." A few were rather colder in their expressions. He had borrowed money from them, and did not offer to return it;

and he was such a generous-minded young man, that they felt a delicacy about calling his attention to it.

"Can you raise a couple of thousand dollars?" was asked of him by a friend, when he was twenty-seven years old. "If you can, I know a first-rate chance to get into business."

"Indeed! What is the nature of it?"

The friend told him all he knew, and he was satisfied that a better offering might never present itself. But two thousand dollars were indispensable.

"Can't you borrow it?" suggested the friend.

"I will try."

"Try your best. You will never again have such an opportunity."

Peyton did try, but in vain. Those who could lend it to him considered him "too good-hearted a fellow" to trust with money; and he was forced to see that tide, which if he could have taken it at the flood, would have led him on to fortune, slowly and steadily recede.

To Merwin the same offer was made. He had fifteen hundred dollars laid by, and easily procured the balance. No one was afraid to trust him with money.

"What a fool I have been!" was the mental exclamation of Peyton, when he learned that his fellow-clerk had been able, with his own earnings, on a salary no larger than his own, to save enough to embrace the golden opportunity which he was forced to pass by. "They call Merwin *mean* and *selfish*—and I am called a *generous fellow*. That means, he has acted like a wise man, and I like a fool, I suppose. I know him better than they do. He is neither mean nor selfish, but careful and prudent, as I ought to have been. His mother is poor, and so is mine. Ah, me!" and the thought of his mother caused him to clasp both hands against his forehead. "I believe two dollars of his salary have been sent weekly to his poor mother. But I have never helped mine a single cent. There is the mean man, and here is the generous one. Fool! fool! wretch! He has fifteen hundred dollars ahead, after having sent his mother one hundred dollars a year for five or six years, and I am over five hundred dollars in debt. A fine, generous fellow, truly!"

The mind of Peyton was, as it should be, disturbed to its very centre. His eyes were fairly opened, and he saw just where he stood, and what he was worth as a generous man.

"They have flattered my weakness," said he, bitterly, "to eat and drink and ride at my expense. It was easy to say, 'how free-hearted he is,' so that I could hear them. A cheap way of enjoying the good things of life, verily! But the end has come to all this. I am just twenty-seven years old to-day; in five years more I shall be thirty-two. My salary is one thousand dollars. I pay one hundred and fifty dollars a year for boarding; one hundred and fifty more shall clothe me and furnish all my spending-money, which shall be precious little. One year from to-day, if I live, I will owe no man a dollar. My kind old mother, whom I have so long neglected, shall hear from me at once—ten dollars every month I dedicate to her. Come what will, nothing shall touch that. After I am clear of debt, I will save all above my necessary expenses, until I get one or two thousand dollars ahead, which shall be in five years. Then I will look out for a golden opportunity, such as Mervin has found. This agreement with myself I solemnly enter into in the sight of heaven, and nothing shall tempt me to violate it."

"Are you going to ride out this afternoon, Peyton?" inquired a young friend, breaking in upon him at this moment.

"Yes, if you'll hire the buggy," was promptly returned.

"I can't afford that."

"Nor I either. How much is your salary?"

"Only a thousand."

"Just what mine is. If you can't, I am sure I cannot."

"Of course, you ought to be the best judge. I knew you rode out almost every afternoon, and liked company."

"Yes, I have done so; but that's past. I have been a 'fine, generous fellow,' long enough to get in debt and mar my prospects for life, perhaps; but I am going to assume a new character. No doubt the very ones who have had so many rides, oyster suppers, and theatre tickets at my expense, will all at once discover that I am as mean and selfish as Mervin; but it's no great odds. I only wish I had been as truly noble and generous in the right quarters as he has been."

"You are in a strange humour to-day."

"I am in a changed humour. That it is so very strange, I do not see—unless for me to think wisely is strange, and perhaps it is."

"Well, all I have to say is, that I, for one, do not blame you, even if I do lose a fine ride into the country now and then," was the frank response.

Peyton went to work in the matter of reform in right good earnest, but he found it hard work; old habits and inclinations were very strong. Still he had some strength of mind, and he brought this into as vigorous exercise as it was possible for him to do, mainly with success, but sometimes with gentle lapses into self-indulgence.

His mother lived in a neighbouring town, and was in humble circumstances. She supported herself by keeping a shop for the sale of various little articles. The old lady sat behind her counter, one afternoon, sewing, and thinking of her only son.

"Ah, me!" she sighed, letting her hands fall wearily in her lap, "I thought Henry would have done something for himself long before this; but he is a wild, free-hearted boy, and I suppose spends every thing as he goes along, just as his father did. I'm afraid he will never do any thing for himself. It is a long time since he wrote home. Ah, me!"

And the mother lifted her work again, and strained her dimmed eyes over it.

"Here's a letter for you at last, Mother Peyton," said the well-known voice of the postman, breaking in upon her just at this moment. "That boy of yours don't write home as often as he used to."

"A letter from Henry! Oh, that is pleasant! Dear boy! he doesn't forget his mother."

"No, one would think not," muttered the postman, as he walked away, "considering how often he writes to her."

With trembling hands, Mrs. Peyton broke the seal; a bank-bill crumpled in her fingers as she opened the letter. A portion of its contents was:

"DEAR MOTHER—I have had some very serious thoughts of late about my way of living. You know I never liked to be considered mean; this led me to be, what seemed to everybody, very generous. Everybody was pleased to eat, and drink, and ride at my expense; but no one seemed inclined to let me do the same at his expense. I have been getting a good salary for six or seven years, and, for a part of that time, as much as a thousand dollars. I am ashamed to say that I have not a farthing laid by; nay, what is worse, I owe a good many little bills. But, dear mother, I think I have come fairly to my senses. I have come to a resolution not to spend a dollar foolishly; thus far I have been able to keep my promise to myself, and, by the help of heaven, I mean to keep it to the end. My first thought, on seeing my folly, was of my shameful disregard to my mother's condition. In this letter are ten dollars. Every month you will receive from me a like sum—more, if you need it. As soon as I can lay by a couple of thousand dollars, I will look around for some means of entering into business, and, as soon after as possible, make provision for you, that your last days may be spent in ease and comfort."

"God bless the dear boy!" exclaimed Mrs. Peyton, dropping the letter, while the tears gushed from her eyes. The happy mother wept long for joy. With her trembling hand she wrote a reply, and urged him, by the tenderest and most sacred considerations, to keep to his good resolutions.

At the end of a year Peyton examined his affairs, and found himself freed from debt; but there were nearly one hundred dollars for which he could not account. He puzzled over it for one or two evenings, and made out over fifty dollars spent foolishly.

"No doubt the rest of it will have to be passed to that account," said he, at last, half angry with himself. "I'll have to watch closer than this. At the end of the next year, I'll not be in doubt about where a hundred dollars have gone."

It was but rarely, now, that you would hear the name of Peyton mentioned. Before, everybody said he was a "fine, generous fellow;" everybody praised him. Now he seemed to be forgotten, or esteemed of no consideration. He felt this; but he had started to accomplish a certain end, and he had sufficient strength of mind not to be driven from his course.

"Have you seen Peyton of late?" I asked, some two years after this change in his habits. I spoke to one of his old intimate associates.

"No, not for a month of Sundays," was his lightly-spoken reply. "What a remarkable change has passed over him! Once, he used to be a fine, generous fellow—his heart was in his hand; but now he is as penurious as a miser, and even more selfish: he will neither give nor take. If you happen to be walking with him, and, after waiting as long as decency will permit to be asked to step in somewhere for refreshments, you propose something, he meets you with—'No, I thank you, I am not dry,' or hungry, as the case may be. It's downright savage, it is!"

"This is a specimen of the way in which the world estimates men," said I to myself, after separating from the individual who complained thus of Peyton. "The world is wonderfully impartial in its judgment of men's conduct!"

At the end of five years from the time Peyton reformed his loose habits, he had saved up and placed out at interest the sum of two thousand dollars; and this, after having sent to his mother, regularly, ten dollars every month during the whole period. The fact that he had saved so much was not suspected by any. It was supposed that he had laid up some money, but no one thought he had over four or five hundred dollars.

"I wish you had about three thousand dollars," said Merwin to him, one day. Merwin's business had turned out well. In five years, he had cleared over twenty thousand dollars.

"Why?" asked Peyton.

"I know a first-rate chance for you."

"Indeed. Where?"

"There is a very good business that has been fairly established, and is now languishing for want of a little capital. The man who has made it will take a partner if he can bring in three thousand dollars, which would make the whole concern easy, perfectly safe, and sure of success."

"It's more than I have," returned Peyton, in a voice that was slightly sad.

"So I supposed," Merwin said.

"Although such needn't have been the case, if I had acted as wisely as you through life."

"It's never too late to mend our ways, you know."

"True. But a year mis-spent, is a whole year lost. No matter how hard we strive, we can never make it up. To the day of our death, there will be one year deficient in the sum of life's account."

"A just remark, no doubt. How much would every man save, if he would take good care not only of his years, but of his weeks and days! The sum of life is made up of small aggregations."

"And so the sum of a man's fortune. A dollar mis-spent is a dollar lost, and never can be regained. You say that it will require three thousand dollars to admit a partner into the business of which you just spoke?"

"Yes. Nothing less will do."

"I have but two thousand."

"Have you so much, Peyton?" said Merwin, with a brightening face.

"I have."

"Right glad am I to hear it. I only wish that I could furnish you with a thousand more. But it is out of my power entirely. Our business requires the use of every dollar we have; and it would not be just to my partner to draw out so large a sum for the purpose of assisting a friend in whom he can feel no interest."

"No, of course not. I neither ask nor expect it. I will wait a little longer. Something else will offer."

"But nothing so really advantageous as this. Let me see. I think I might get you five hundred dollars, if you could borrow as much more."

"That I cannot do. I never asked a favour of any one in my life."

"Though you have dispensed thousands."

"Foolishly perhaps. But no matter. I will wait."

A week afterward, Peyton, who dismissed all thought of embracing the proposed offer of going in business, paid a visit to his mother. He had not seen her for a year. She was still cheerful, active, and retained her usual good health.

"I think it time you gave up this shop, mother," said he to her. "You are too old now to be working so closely. I've got something saved up for a rainy day, in case any thing should go wrong with me for a time. You will give up this shop, won't you?"

"No, Henry; not yet. I am still able to help myself, and so long as I am able, I wish to do it. If you have saved any thing, you had better keep it until an opportunity for going into business offers."

"Such a chance has just presented itself. But I hadn't capital enough."

"How much have you saved?"

"Two thousand dollars."

"So much? How much is required?"

"Three thousand dollars."

"And you have but two?"

"That is all—though a friend did offer to get me five hundred more. But twenty-five hundred is not sufficient. There must be three thousand."

Mrs. Peyton made no reply. She sat a few minutes, and then arose and went up-stairs. In about ten minutes she came down, and approaching her son, with a warm glow of pleasure upon her face, placed a small roll in his hands, saying as she did so—

"There is all you need, my son. The money you sent me so regularly for the last five years, I have kept untouched for some such moment as this. I did not feel that I needed it. Take it back, and start fairly in the world. In a few more years I may need rest, as life draws nearer to a close. Then I trust you will be in circumstances so good that I needn't feel myself a burden to you."

"A burden? Dear mother! Do not speak of ever being a burden to me," said the young man, embracing his parent with tearful emotion. "No—no," and he pushed back her hand; "I cannot take that money. It is yours. I will not risk in business the little treasure you have saved up so carefully. I may not succeed. No—no!" and he still pushed back his mother's hand—"it is of no use—I cannot—I *will* not take it!"

The roll of money fell to the floor.

"It is yours, Henry, not mine," urged the mother. "I did not stand in need of it."

"Your son owed you much more than that. He was wrong that he did not double the amount to you, in order to make up for former years of neglect. No—no—I tell you, mother, I cannot take your money. Nothing would tempt me to do it. I will wait a little longer. Other opportunities will soon offer."

It was in vain that Mrs. Peyton urged her son, until her distress of mind became so great that he was almost forced to receive the money she pushed upon him—although, in doing so, it was with the intention of leaving it behind him when he returned to the city. But the deep satisfaction evinced by his mother, on his consenting to take it, was of a kind that he did not feel it would be right for him to do violence to. When he did return to the city, he could not find it in his heart to leave the money, just six hundred dollars, on the table in the little room where he slept, as he had at first resolved to do. He took it with him; but with the intention of investing it for her in some safe security.

When he again met Merwin, he was urged so strongly to make an effort to raise the capital requisite to become a partner in the business that had been named to him, that after some severe struggles with himself, he at last consented to use the money he had brought home with him. His friend loaned him four hundred dollars to make up the required sum.

The business succeeded beyond his expectations. In a few years he was able to marry, and live in a very comfortable style. He would hear none of the objections urged by his mother against living with him, but shut up her shop in spite of her remonstrances, and brought her to the city. No one who saw her during the remaining ten years of her life would have called her unhappy.

I know Peyton still. He is not now, by general reputation, "a fine, generous fellow." But he is a good citizen, a good husband, and a good father; and was a good son while his mother lived with him. He has won the means of really benefiting others, and few are more willing than he is to do it, when it can be done in the right way. He is "generous" still—but wisely so.

Words for the Wise

TAKING IT FOR GRANTED.

MR. EVERTON was the editor and publisher of the——Journal, and, like too many occupying his position, was not on the best terms in the world with certain of his contemporaries of the same city. One morning, on opening the paper from a rival office, he found an article therein, which appeared as a communication, that pointed to him so directly as to leave no room for mistake as to the allusions that were made.

Of course, Mr. Everton was considerably disturbed by the occurrence, and thoughts of retaliation arose in his mind. The style was not that of the editor, and so, though he felt incensed at that personage for admitting the article, he went beyond him, and cast about in his mind for some clue that would enable him to identify the writer. In this he did not long find himself at a loss. He had a man in his employment who possessed all the ability necessary to write the article, and upon whom, for certain reasons, he soon fixed the origin of the attack.

"Have you seen that article in the Gazette?" asked an acquaintance, who came into Everton's office while he sat with the paper referred to still in his hand.

"I have," replied Everton, compressing his lips.

"Well, what do you think of it?"

"It'll do no harm, of course; but that doesn't touch the malice of the writer."

"No."

"Nor make him any the less base at heart."

"Do you know the author?"

"I believe so."

"Who is he?"

"My impression is, that Ayres wrote it."

"Ayres?"

"Yes."

"Why, he is indebted to you for his bread!"

"I know he is, and that makes his act one of deeper baseness."

"What could have induced him to be guilty of such a thing?"

"That's just what I've been trying to study out, and I believe I understand it all fully. Some six months ago, he asked me to sign a recommendation for his appointment to a vacant clerkship in one of our banks. I told him that I would do so with pleasure, only that my nephew was an applicant, and I had already given him my name. He didn't appear to like this, which I thought very unreasonable, to say the least of it."

"Why, the man must be insane! How could he expect you to sign the application of two men for the same place? Especially, how could he expect you to give him a preference over your own nephew?"

"Some men are strangely unreasonable."

"We don't live long in this world ere becoming cognisant of that fact."

"And for this he has held a grudge against you, and now takes occasion to revenge himself."

"So it would seem. I know of nothing else that he can have against me. I have uniformly treated him with kindness and consideration."

"There must be something radically base in his character."

"I'm afraid there is."

"I wouldn't have such a man in my employment."

Everton shrugged his shoulders and elevated his eyebrows, but said nothing.

"A man who attempts thus to injure you in your business by false representations, will not hesitate to wrong you in other ways," said the acquaintance.

"A very natural inference," replied Everton. "I'm sorry to have to think so badly of Ayres; but, as you say, a man who would, in so base a manner, attack another, would not hesitate to do him an injury if a good opportunity offered."

"And it's well for you to think of that."

"True. However, I do not see that he has much chance to do me an ill-turn where he is. So far, I must do him the justice to say that he is faithful in the discharge of all his duties."

"He knows that his situation depends upon this."

"Of course. His own interest prompts him to do right here; but when an opportunity to stab me in the dark offers, he embraces it. He did not, probably, imagine that I would see the hand that held the dagger."

"No."

"But I am not so blind as he imagined. Well, such work must not be permitted to go unpunished."

"It ought not to be. When a man indulges his ill-nature towards one individual with entire impunity, he soon gains courage for extended attacks, and others become sharers in the result of his vindictiveness. It is a duty that a man owes the community to let all who maliciously wrong him feel the consequences due to their acts."

"No doubt you are right; and, if I keep my present mind, I shall let my particular friend Mr. Ayres feel that it is not always safe to stab even in the dark."

The more Mr. Everton thought over the matter, the more fully satisfied was he that Ayres had made the attack upon him. This person was engaged as reporter and assistant editor of his newspaper, at a salary of ten dollars a week. He had a family, consisting of a wife and four children, the expense of whose maintenance rather exceeded than came within his income, and small accumulations of debt were a natural result.

Everton had felt some interest in this man, who possessed considerable ability as a writer; he saw that he had a heavy weight upon him, and often noticed that he looked anxious and dejected. On the very day previous to the appearance of the article above referred to, he had been thinking of him with more than usual interest, and had actually meditated an increase of salary as a compensation for more extended services. But that was out of the question now. The wanton and injurious attack which had just appeared shut up all his bowels of compassion, and so far from meditating the conferring of a benefit upon Ayres, he rather inclined to a dismissal of the young man from his establishment. The longer he dwelt upon it, the more inclined was he to pursue this course, and, finally, he made up his mind to take some one else in his place. One day, after some struggles with himself, he said, "Mr. Ayres, if you can suit yourself in a place, I wish you would do so in the course of the next week or two."

The young man looked surprised, and the blood instantly suffused his face.

"Have I not given you satisfaction?" inquired Ayres.

"Yes—yes—I have no fault to find with you," replied Mr. Everton, with some embarrassment in his air. "But I wish to bring in another person who has some claims on me."

In this, Mr. Everton rather exceeded the truth. His equivocation was not manly, and Ayres was deceived by it into the inference of a reason for his dismissal foreign to the true one.

"Oh, very well," he replied, coldly. "If you wish another to take my place, I will give it up immediately."

Mr. Everton bowed with a formal air, and the young man, who felt hurt at his manner, and partly stunned by the unexpected announcement that he must give up his situation, retired at once.

On the next day, the Gazette contained another article, in which there was even a plainer reference to Mr. Everton than before, and it exhibited a bitterness of spirit that was vindictive. He was no longer in doubt as to the origin of these attacks, if he had been previously. In various parts of this last article, he could detect the particular style of Ayres.

"I see that fellow is at work on you again," said the person with whom he had before conversed on the subject.

"Yes; but, like the viper, I think he is by this time aware that he is biting on a file."

"Ah! Have you dismissed him from your service?"

"Yes, sir."

"You have served him right. No man who attempted to injure me should eat my bread. What did he say?"

"Nothing. What could he say? When I told him to find himself another place as quickly as possible, his guilt wrote itself in his countenance."

"Has he obtained a situation?"

"I don't know; and, what is more, don't care."

"I hope he has, for the sake of his family. It's a pity that they should suffer for his evil deeds."

"I didn't think of them, or I might not have dismissed him; but it is done now, and there the matter rests."

And there Mr. Everton let it rest, so far as Ayres was concerned. The individual obtained in his place had been, for some years, connected with the press as news collector and paragraph writer. His name was Tompkins. He was not a general favourite, and had never been very highly regarded by Mr. Everton; but he must have some one to fill the place made vacant by the removal of Ayres, and Tompkins was the most available person to be had. There was a difference in the Journal after Tompkins took the place of assistant editor, and a very perceptible difference; it was not for the better.

About three months after Mr. Everton had dismissed Ayres from his establishment, a gentleman said to him,

"I am told that the young man who formerly assisted in your paper is in very destitute circumstances."

"Ayres?"

"Yes. That is his name."

"I am sorry to hear it. I wish him no ill; though he tried to do me all the harm he could."

"I am sorry to hear that. I always had a good opinion of him; and come, now, to see if I can't interest you in his favour."

Everton shook his head.

"I don't wish to have any thing to do with him."

"It pains me to hear you speak so. What has he done to cause you to feel so unkindly towards him?"

"He attacked me in another newspaper, wantonly, at the very time he was employed in my office."

"Indeed!"

"Yes, and in a way to do me a serious injury."

"That is bad. Where did the attack appear?"

"In the Gazette."

"Did you trace it to him?"

"Yes; or, rather, it bore internal evidence that enabled me to fix it upon him unequivocally."

"Did you charge it upon him?"

"No. I wished to have no quarrel with him, although he evidently tried to get up one with me. I settled the matter by notifying him to leave my employment."

"You are certain that he wrote the article?"

"Oh, yes; positive."

And yet the very pertinence of the question threw a doubt into the mind of Mr. Everton.

The gentleman with whom he was conversing on retiring went to the office of the Gazette, with the editor of which he was well acquainted.

"Do you remember," said he, "an attack on Mr. Everton, which, some time ago, appeared in your paper?"

The editor reflected a few moments, and then replied:

"A few months since, two or three articles were published in the Gazette that did refer to Everton in not a very kind manner."

"Do you know the author?"

"Yes."

"Have you any reasons for wishing to conceal his name?"

"None at all. They were written by a young man who was then in my office, named Tompkins."

"You are certain of this?"

"I am certain that he brought them to me in his own manuscript."

"Everton suspected a man named Ayres to be the author."

"His assistant editor at the time?"

"Yes; and what is more, discharged him from his employment on the strength of this suspicion."

"What injustice! Ayres is as innocent as you are."

"I am glad to hear it. The consequences to the poor man have been very sad. He has had no regular employment since, and his family are now suffering for even the common necessaries of life."

"That is very bad. Why didn't he deny the charge when it was made against him?"

"He was never accused. Everton took it for granted that he was guilty, and acted from this erroneous conclusion."

"What a commentary upon hasty judgments! Has he no employment now?"

"None."

"Then I will give him a situation. I know him to be competent for the place I wish filled; and I believe he will be faithful."

Here the interview ceased, and the gentleman who had taken the pains to sift out the truth returned to Everton's office.

"Well," said he, on entering, "I believe I have got to the bottom of this matter."

"What matter?" asked Everton, looking slightly surprised.

"The matter of Ayres's supposed attack upon you."

"Why do you say supposed?"

"Because it was only supposed. Ayres didn't write the article of which you complain."

"How do you know?"

"I've seen the editor of the Gazette."

"Did he say that Ayres was not the author?"

"He did."

"Who wrote it then?"

"A man named Tompkins, who was at the time employed in his office."

Everton sprang from his chair as if he had been stung.

"Tompkins!" he exclaimed.

"So he says."

"Can it be possible! And I have the viper in my employment."

"You have?"

"Yes; he has filled the place of Ayres nearly ever since the latter was dismissed from my office."

"Then you have punished the innocent and rewarded the guilty."

"So much for taking a thing for granted," said Everton, as he moved, restlessly, about the floor of his office.

So soon as the editor of the——Journal was alone, he sent for Tompkins, who was in another part of the building. As the young man entered his office, he said to him, in a sharp, abrupt manner,—

"Do you remember certain articles against me that appeared in the Gazette a few months ago?"

The young man, whose face became instantly red as scarlet, stammered out that he did remember them.

"And you wrote them?"

"Ye—ye—yes; bu—but I have regretted it since, very much."

"You can put on your hat and leave my employment as quickly as you please," said Mr. Everton, angrily. He had little control of himself, and generally acted from the spur of the occasion.

Tompkins, thus severely punished for going out of the way to attack a man against whom he entertained a private grudge, beat a hasty retreat, and left Mr. Everton in no very comfortable frame of mind.

On being so unceremoniously dismissed from employment, Mr. Ayres, who was by nature morbidly sensitive, shrank into himself, and experienced a most painful feeling of helplessness. He was not of a cheerful, confident, hopeful disposition. He could not face the world, and battle for his place in it, like many other men. A little thing discouraged him. To be thrust out of his place so unceremoniously—to be turned off for another, stung him deeply. But the worst of all was, the supply of bread for his family was cut off, and no other resource was before him.

From that time, for three months, his earnings never went above the weekly average of five dollars; and he hardly knew on one day where he was to obtain employment for the next. His wife, though in poor health, was obliged to dispense with all assistance, and perform, with her own hands, the entire work of the family. This wore her down daily, and Ayres saw her face growing thinner, and her step becoming more feeble, without the power to lighten her burdens.

Thus it went on from week to week. Sometimes, the unhappy man would grow desperate, and, under this feeling, force himself to make applications—to him humiliating—for employment at a fair compensation. But he was always unsuccessful.

Sickness at last smote the frame of his wife. She had borne up as long as strength remained, but the weight was too heavy, and she sank under it.

Sickness and utter destitution came together. Ayres had not been able to get any thing at all to do for several days, and money and food were both exhausted. A neighbour, hearing of this, had sent in a basket of provisions. But Ayres could not touch it. His sensitive pride of independence was not wholly extinguished. The children ate, and he blessed the hand of the giver for their sakes; yet, even while he did so, a feeling of weakness and humiliation brought tears to his eyes. His spirits were broken, and he folded his arms in impotent despair. While sitting wrapt in the gloomiest feelings, there came a knock at his door. One of the children opened it, and a lad came in with a note in his hand. On breaking the seal, he found it to be from the publisher of the Gazette, who offered him a permanent situation at twelve dollars a week. So overcome was he by such unexpected good fortune, that he with difficulty controlled his feelings before the messenger. Handing the note to his wife, who was lying on the bed, he turned to a table and wrote a hasty answer, accepting the place, and stating that he would be down in the course of an hour. As the boy departed, he looked towards his wife. She had turned her face to the wall, and was weeping violently.

"It was very dark, Jane," said Ayres, as he took her hand, bending over her at the same time and kissing her forehead, "very dark; but the light is breaking."

Scarcely had the boy departed, when a heavy rap at the door disturbed the inmates of that humble dwelling.

"Mr. Everton!" exclaimed Ayres in surprise, as he opened the door.

"I want you to come back to my office," said the visitor, speaking in a slightly agitated voice. "I never ought to have parted with you. But to make some amends, your wages shall be twelve dollars a week. And here," handing out some money as he spoke, "is your pay for a month in advance."

"I thank you for the offer, Mr. Everton," replied the young man, "but the publisher of the Gazette has already tendered me a situation, and I have accepted it."

The countenance of Mr. Everton fell.

"When did this occur?" he inquired.

"His messenger has been gone only a moment."

Mr. Everton stood for a few seconds irresolute, while his eyes took in the images of distress and destitution apparent on every hand. His feelings no one need envy. If his thoughts had been uttered at the time, his words would have been, "This is the work of my hands!" He still held out the money, but Ayres did not touch it.

"What does he offer you?" he at length asked.

"Twelve dollars a week," was replied.

"I will make it fifteen."

"I thank you," said Ayres, in answer to this, "but my word is passed, and I cannot recall it."

"Then take this as a loan, and repay me when you can."

Saying this, Everton tossed a small roll of bank bills upon the floor, at the feet of the young man, adding as he did so—"And if you are ever in want of a situation, come to me."

He then hurriedly retired, with what feelings the reader may imagine.

The reason for this suddenly awakened interest on the part of Mr. Everton, Ayres did not know until he entered the service of his new employer. He had the magnanimity to forgive him, notwithstanding all he had suffered; and he is now back again in his service on a more liberal salary than he ever before enjoyed.

Mr. Everton is now exceedingly careful how he takes any thing for granted.

LOVE AND LAW.

LLOYD TOMLINSON was a Virginia gentleman of the old school, and held high notions on the kindred subjects of social rank and family distinctions. His ancestors were connected with English families of some renown, and had figured in history as Cavaliers, during the troublesome times of Charles I. Portraits of the most noted of these were hung upon the walls in Mr. Tomlinson's fine old mansion, and it was with pride that he often referred to them and related the story of each. But such stories were generally wound up by an expression of regret for the sad deteriorations that were going on in this country.

"A man like that," he would sometimes say, pointing to the picture of a stern old Cavalier, "is rarely, if ever, met with, and in a little while there will be no living representative of such—at least not in America, where all social distinctions are rapidly disappearing. In fact, we have scarcely any thing left, even now, but the shadow of a true aristocracy, and that is only to be found in Virginia. At the North, mere wealth makes a man a gentleman; and this new invention of these degenerate times is fast being adopted even here in the 'Old Dominion.' But it won't do—unless a man is born and bred a gentleman, he never can become one."

It was no use to argue with the rigid old Virginian about the aristocracy of virtue, or the aristocracy of mind; he scouted at the idea, and reiterated, with added emphasis, that only he who was born of gentle blood could be a gentleman.

The family of Mr. Tomlinson, which had consisted of his wife, two sons, and two daughters, was, at the time our story opens, composed of only two members, himself and his youngest child, Edith, now in her nineteenth year. Death had taken all but one.

Edith, though born and bred a lady, her father observed, with pain, did not set a high value upon the distinction, and at last actually refused to receive the addresses of a young man who came of pure old English blood, and was a thorough gentleman in the eyes of Mr. Tomlinson, because she liked neither his principles, habits, nor general character, while she looked with favour upon the advances of a young attorney, named Denton, whose father, a small farmer in Essex county, had nothing higher than honesty and manly independence of which to boast.

The young gentleman of pure blood was named Allison. He was the last representative of an old family, and had come into possession, on attaining his majority, of a large landed estate immediately adjoining that owned by Mr. Tomlinson. The refusal of Edith to receive his addresses aroused in him an unhappy spirit, which he cherished until it inspired him with thoughts of retaliation. The means were in his hands. There existed an old, but not legally adjusted question, about the title to a thousand acres of land lying between the estates of Mr. Tomlinson and Mr. Allison, which had, more than fifty years before, been settled by the principal parties thereto on the basis of a fair division, without the delay, vexation, expense, and bitterness of a prolonged lawsuit. By this division, the father of Mr. Tomlinson retained possession of five hundred acres, and the grandfather of Mr. Allison of the other five hundred. The former had greatly improved the portion into the full possession of which he had come, as it was by far the most beautiful and fertile part of his estate. His old residence was torn down, and a splendid mansion erected on a commanding eminence within the limits of this old disputed land, at a cost of nearly eighty thousand dollars, and the whole of the five hundred acres gradually brought into a high state of cultivation. To meet the heavy outlay for all this, other and less desirable portions of the estate were sold, until, finally, only about three hundred acres of the original Tomlinson property remained.

Mr. Lloyd Tomlinson, as he advanced in years, and felt the paralyzing effects of the severe afflictions he had suffered, lost much of the energy he had possessed in his younger days. There was a gradual diminution in the number of hogsheads of tobacco and bushels of corn and wheat that went into Richmond from his plantation annually; and there was also a steady decrease in the slave population with which he was immediately surrounded. From a hundred and fifty, his slaves had decreased, until he only owned thirty, and with them did little more than make his yearly expenses. Field after field had been abandoned, and left to a fertile undergrowth of pines or scrubby oaks, until there were few signs of cultivation, except within the limits of two or three hundred acres of the rich lands contiguous to his dwelling.

Henry Denton, the young attorney to whom allusion has been made, had become deeply enamoured with Edith Tomlinson, who was often met by him in her unaristocratic intercourse with several excellent and highly intelligent families in the neighbourhood. To see her, was for him to love her; but the pride of her father was too well known by him to leave much room for hope that the issue of his passion would be successful, even if so fortunate as to win the heart of the maiden. He was inspired with courage, however, by the evident favour with which she regarded him, and even tempted to address her in language that no woman's ear could mistake—the language of love. Edith listened with a heart full of hope and fear. She had great respect for the character of Denton, which she saw was based upon virtuous principles; and this respect easily changed into love that was true and fervent; but she knew too well her father's deeply-rooted prejudices in favour of rank and family, to hope that the current of her love would run smooth. This proved to be no idle fear. When Henry Denton ventured to approach Mr. Tomlinson on the subject of his love for Edith, the old gentleman received him with great discourtesy.

"Who are you, sir?" he asked, drawing himself proudly up.

"I hardly think you need ask that question," the young man replied. "I am not an entire stranger to you, nor unknown in your neighbourhood."

"But who are you, sir? That is what I ask to know. Who is your father?"

"An honest man, sir." The young man spoke with firmness and dignity.

"Humph! there are plenty of them about. I could marry my daughter to an honest man any day I liked. Old Cato, my coachman, is an honest man; but that is no reason why I should let his son Sam marry Edith. No, my young friend, you cannot connect yourself with my family; be content with the daughter of some honest man like your father."

But the lover was not to be driven off by even such a rude repulse. He tried to argue his case, but Mr. Tomlinson cut the matter short by starting from his seat in great discomposure of mind, and pointing with a trembling hand to a grim picture on the wall, while he thus addressed the young man:—

"That, sir, is the portrait of Sir Edgar Tomlinson, who, by interposing his body between the spear of a Roundhead and his royal master, saved his life at the imminent risk of his own, for which gallant deed he was knighted, and afterwards presented, by royal hands, with a noble bride. When you have done as great a deed, young man, you will be worthy to claim the hand of my daughter—not before!"

Saying this, the excited father turned away and strode from the room, leaving Denton in dismay at the quick and hopeless termination of his conference.

On the next day, the young attorney, who was known to possess fine talents, acuteness, and extensive legal knowledge, was waited upon by Mr. Allison.

"I wish your services, Mr. Denton," said he, "in a suit of great importance that I am about commencing. Here is your retaining fee,"—and he laid upon the table of the lawyer a check for two hundred dollars. "If you gain me my cause, your entire fee will be five thousand dollars."

Allison then went on to state, that Mr. Tomlinson's claim to the five hundred acres next adjoining his (Allison's) plantation, and upon which his mansion stood, was a very doubtful one. That it, in fact, belonged to the Allison estate, and he was going to have the question of rightful ownership fully tested. He furnished the young attorney with documents, data, and every thing required for commencing the suit. Denton asked a week for an examination of the whole matter. At the end of this time, Allison again waited on him.

"Well, sir, what do you think of my case?" he said.

"I think it a doubtful one," was replied. "Still, it is possible you might gain it, as there are one or two strong points in your favour."

"I have not the least doubt of it. At any rate, I am going to give the matter a fair trial. Five hundred acres of such land are worth an effort to gain."

"But you must not forget that, as you will open the question of ownership on the whole tract of one thousand acres, you run the risk of losing the half of which you are now in possession."

"I'm willing to run the risk of losing five hundred acres of uncultivated land in the effort to acquire possession of as large a quantity in a high state of improvement," returned the uncompromising gentleman 'born and bred.' "So you will forthwith make a beginning in the matter."

The young attorney was grave and silent for some time. Then opening a drawer, he took out the check which had been given to him as a retaining fee, and handing it to Allison, said—"I believe, sir, I must decline this case."

"Why so?" quickly asked the young man, a deep flush passing over his brow.

"I do it from principle," was replied. "I find, on examining the whole matter, that your grandfather and the father of Mr. Tomlinson, while in possession of their respective estates, in view of the difficulty there was in settling the precise title of the tract of land, agreed to an equal division of it, which was done in honour and good faith, and I do not think their heirs, on either side, have any right to disturb the arrangement then made."

"I did not ask you to judge the case, but to present it for judgment," said Allison, greatly offended. "You may, perhaps, be sorry for this."

Another member of the bar, less scrupulous about the principles involved in a case, readily undertook the matter; and as the fee, if he proved successful, was to be a large one, opened it immediately.

When Mr. Tomlinson received notice of the fact that this long-settled dispute was again to be revived, he was thrown into a fever of alarm and indignation. The best counsel that could be employed was obtained, and his right to the whole thousand acres vigorously maintained. After a year of delays, occasioned by demurrers, allegations, and all sorts of legal hinderances, made and provided for the vexation of clients, the question came fairly before the court, where it was most ably argued on both sides for some days. When the decision at length came, it was adverse to Mr. Tomlinson.

An appeal was entered, and preparations made for a more vigorous contest in a higher court. Here the matter remained for over a year, when the decision of the first tribunal was confirmed.

Two years of litigation had made sad work with old Mr. Tomlinson; he looked at least ten years older. The same signs of decay appeared in every thing around him; his fields remained uncultivated, the fences were broken down, and cattle strayed where once were acres of grain or other rich products. Slaves and stock had been sold to meet the heavy expenses to which this suit had subjected him, and every thing seemed fast tending towards ruin. Once or twice during the period, Denton again approached him on the subject of Edith, but the proud old aristocrat threw him off even more impatiently than at first.

Edith, too, had changed during this time of trouble; she was rarely seen abroad, and received but few visitors at home. No one saw her smile, unless when her father was present; and then her manner was cheerful, though subdued. It was clear that she was struggling against her own feelings, in the effort to sustain his. Her father had extorted from her a promise never to marry without his consent; this settled the matter for the time between her and Denton, although both remained faithful to each other; they had not met for over a year.

Meantime the cause was carried up still higher, where it remained for two years longer, and then another adverse decision was made. Mr. Tomlinson was in despair; what with court charges, counsel fees, and loss from the diminished productions of his farm, he had sunk in the last four years over fifteen thousand dollars, a portion of which had been raised by mortgage on that part of his estate to which he had an undisputed title, almost equal to the full value of the land.

To the Supreme Court the matter came at last, but the old man had but little hope. In three courts, after a long and patient hearing, the decision had been against him; if it should again be adverse, he would be totally ruined. As it was, so greatly had his means become reduced, that it was with difficulty he could raise sufficient money to pay off the heavy expenses of the last court. The fees of his two attorneys were yet unsettled, and he feared, greatly, that he should not be able to induce more than one of them to attend at the Supreme Court. On the other side, money was expended freely, and the most energetic counsel that money could command enlisted. The fact was, the principal reason why Mr. Tomlinson had failed in each of the three trials that had already taken place lay in the superior tact, activity, and ability of the adverse counsel.

The anxiously looked-for period at length came, and Mr. Tomlinson made preparations for leaving home to meet the final issue, after nearly five years of most cruel litigation.

"Dear father!" said Edith, as they were about to separate. She spoke with forced calmness, while a faint smile of encouragement played about her lips; her voice was low and tender. "Dear father, do not let this matter press too heavily upon you; I have a hope that all will come out right. I do not know why, but I feel as if this dreadful blow will not be permitted to fall. Be calm, be brave, dear father! even the worst can be borne."

The maiden's voice began to quiver, even while she uttered hopeful words. Mr. Tomlinson, whose own heart was full, bent down and kissed her hurriedly. When she looked up, he was gone. How fast the tears flowed, as she stood alone on the spot where they had just parted!

A few hours after the father had left, a gentleman called and asked to see Edith. On entering the room where he had been shown by the servant, she found a young man whose countenance she had never seen before. He. made known his business after a few embarrassing preliminaries, which proved to be an overture of peace from Allison, if she would accept the offer of marriage he had made her five years previously. After hearing the young man patiently through, Edith replied, in a firm voice—"Tell Mr. Allison that there is no evil in this world or the next that I would consider greater than a marriage with him."

He attempted to urge some considerations upon her, but she raised her hand, and said, in a tone of decision, "You have my answer, sir; take it to your principal."

The young man bowed, and withdrew in silence. He felt awed beneath the steady eye, calm face, and resolute voice of the maiden, crushed almost to the earth as she was.

When Mr. Tomlinson arrived at the capital, he found neither of his counsel there, although the case was expected to be reached on the succeeding day. On the next morning he received a note from one of them, which stated that illness would prevent his attending. The other attorney was prepared to go on with the case, but he was by far the weakest of the two.

On the opposite side there was the strongest possible array, both as to number and talents. Mr. Tomlinson felt that his case was hopeless. On the first day the prosecution argued their case with great ability. On the second day, the claims of Mr. Tomlinson were presented, with even less point and tact than before; it was clear that the advocate either considered the case a bad one, or had lost all interest in it. The other side followed with increased confidence, and, it was plain, made a strong impression upon the court. A feeble rejoinder was given to this, but it produced little or no effect.

Just at this crisis, an individual, not before particularly noticed by Mr. Tomlinson, arose and addressed the court. His opening remarks showed him to be familiar with the whole subject, and his tone and manner exhibited a marked degree of confidence. It was soon apparent which side of the case he had taken; if by nothing else, by the frown that settled upon the brow of Allison. He was a young man, tall and well made, with a strong, clear voice, and a fine command of language. The position in which he stood concealed so much of his face from Mr. Tomlinson, that the latter could not make out whether it was one with which he was familiar or not. The voice he had heard before.

The volunteer advocate, after having occupied the court for an hour, during which time he had shown a most minute and accurate knowledge of the matter in dispute, gave the whole question a new aspect. During the second hour that his argument was continued, in which precedent after precedent, not before introduced, were brought forward, bearing a direct application to the case under review, the court exhibited the most marked attention. When he concluded, all present saw hope for the old Virginian.

This new and unexpected champion in the cause aroused the counsel of Allison to another and more determined effort; but he tore their arguments into ribands, and set off their authorities with an overwhelming array of decisions directly in the teeth of those they introduced bearing upon their side of the question. It was wonderful to observe his perfect familiarity with the whole matter in dispute, the law bearing upon it, and the decisions of courts in this country and England, that could in any way throw light upon it, far outstripping the learned advocates on both sides, who had been at work upon the case for five years.

During the time this brilliant champion was fighting his battle for him in the last defensible position he could ever obtain, Mr. Tomlinson remained as if fixed to the spot where he was sitting, yet with his mind entirely active. He saw, he felt that there was hope for him; that this heaven-sent advocate, whoever he was, would save him from ruin. At last the case closed, and the court announced that its decision would be given in the morning.

"Who is he?" Mr. Tomlinson heard some one ask of his persecutor, as the young man closed his last and most brilliant effort.

With an imprecation uttered between his teeth, he replied, "One that refused to take my side, although I offered him a fee of five thousand dollars if successful."

"What is his name?"

"Denton."

"Pity you couldn't have secured him."

Mr. Tomlinson heard no more. He turned his eyes upon the young man he had three times rudely repulsed, but he could not see his face; he was bending over and arranging some papers. The announcement of the court, in regard to the time when a decision was to be made, drew his attention from him. When he again sought the young attorney, he was gone.

Nearly a week of most distressing suspense was suffered by Edith. Every day she heard from her father, but all was doubt and despondency, until there came a letter announcing the sudden appearance of a volunteer advocate, who had changed the whole aspect of affairs, and created the most lively hopes of success. Who he was, the letter did not say.

During the morning that succeeded the one on which this letter was received, Edith wandered about the house like a restless spirit. The decision had been made on the day previous, and in a few hours her father would be home. What intelligence would he bring? Whenever she asked herself that question, her heart trembled. Twenty times had she been to the highest windows in the house to look far away where the road wound down a distant hill, to see if the carriage were coming, although she knew two hours must elapse before her father could possibly arrive.

At last the long and anxiously looked-for object came in sight, winding along the road far in the distance. Soon it passed from view, and she waited breathlessly, until it should appear at a nearer point. Again it met her eyes, and again disappeared. At last it reached the long avenue of poplars that lined the carriage-way leading up to the house; the horses were coming at a rapid speed. Edith could not breathe in the rooms—the atmosphere was oppressive. She went into the porch, and, leaning against or rather clinging to one of the pillars, stood almost gasping for breath. The suspense she suffered was awful; but certainty soon came. The carriage whirled rapidly into its position before the door, and Mr. Tomlinson sprang from it as agile as a boy. He had merely time to say—

"All is safe!" when Edith sank into his arms, unable longer to stand.

"And here is our noble champion," he added, as another stood by his side.

Edith opened her eyes, that she had closed in the excess of joy; the face of her lover was near her. She looked up at him for a moment, and then closed them again; but now the tears came stealing through her shut lids.

The young lawyer had gained two suits in one. Three months afterwards Edith was his bride, and the dowry was the five hundred acres of land from the estate of Allison, awarded to her father by the Supreme Court.

THE END.